Deep Tissue

Jeff Tapia

Livingston Press
The University of West Alabama

Copyright © 2012 Jeff Tapia
All rights reserved, including electronic text
isbn 13: 978-1-60489-088-4 library binding
isbn 13: 978-1-60489-089-1 trade paper
Library of Congress Control Number 2012930428
Printed on acid-free paper.
Printed in the United States of America by
United Graphics

Hardcover binding by: Heckman Bindery
Typesetting and page layout: Joe Taylor
Proofreading: Joe Taylor, Stephanie Murray,
Tricia Taylor, Jim Carroll, Danielle Harvey, Eadie Caver,
Nelson Simms
Cover design: Jana Vukovic

Previously Published Acknowledgements:

The author thanks the editors and staff of the literary journals where these stories originally appeared: "Tammy," *Sucarnochee Review*; Deep Tissue," *JMWW*; Horns Overflowing," *Tarpaulin Sky*; "An Emu Is like an Ostrich," *Pendeldyboz*.

This is a work of fiction. Any resemblance
to persons living or dead is coincidental.
Livingston Press is part of The University of West Alabama,
and thereby has non-profit status.
Donations are tax-deductible:
brothers and sisters, we need 'em.

first edition
6 5 4 3 3 2 1

Deep Tissue

Table of Contents

Deep Tissue	1
Tammy	20
Horns Overflowing	27
A Colt	38
Pie	44
The Body Manager	53
Fear's	62
The Grumbler	71
An Emu Is Like an Ostrich	80
Home Theater	84
The Dark Continent	91
Nachtmusik	129

Deep Tissue

This happened. Ken's left arm was playing Velcro darts against Ken's right arm. Ken's right arm was beating Ken's left arm. Ken's left arm hardly ever won. It was bad. Sometimes Ken's right arm smeared Ken's left arm bad. He was keeping score on a pad of paper. It had the name of his travel agency at the top. Ken's travel agency was called Ken's Travel. Ken's travel agency was going out of business. Ken sat at his desk all day long. Sometimes he played darts. Ken was sitting in his deluxe business chair. It was the ultimate in office comfort. It had multifunction knobs to modify the angle of the back and control the forward tilt. There were not any customers in Ken's office. The lights were not even on. It was sunny outside. It was not very dark inside. The office had big windows. Houseplants were in the windows. One was a rubber plant. They told Ken rubber plants were perfect for beginners. It had glossy, leathery, large leaves. They were oblong to oval. Ken threw another dart. It stuck to the board. Ken wrote down 40. It was what his arm got. Ken had once been 40 himself. It was not that long ago. Ken was over 40 now. Ken made a stick figure out of the 0 in the 40. The 0 was the head. The face in the 0 was in anguish. Ken drew a box around the stick figure. The stick figure was trapped in the box. That signified Ken. The stick figure's hands and feet were out of proportion. They were too big. Ken's travel agency was located right next to a pet supplies shop. Next to the pet supplies shop was a Hallmark's. Next to that was

Shelly's hair salon. She cut hair. Next to Shelly's hair salon was Mail Boxes Etc. Mail Boxes Etc. had recently joined forces with UPS and was now the world's largest retail shipping, postal, and business services franchise company. Next to that was the huge supermarket where everybody went. Ken liked their donuts. He thought they tasted good. He bought a chocolate long john there every morning. The bakery knew him there. Reuben juggled dough balls sometimes when Ken asked him to. Ken did not care what was on the other side of the supermarket. Ken did not give a shit. Ken threw another dart. It was his left arm's turn. It barely stuck to the board. It was hanging by one Velcro. That was like Ken, too. Ken could not take it. Ken was just hanging there. Ken put down his right arm's last dart. It no longer mattered. Ken's left arm could not even catch up with a bull's eye. It was hard to get a bull's eye. The bull's eye was small and red. Ken stopped playing. It was still early in the morning. Then Ken lost himself in his screen saver. He zombied out. Ken watched the sun set over and over. It was in a tropical setting. Ken's day was just beginning. Ken's day was not to end for a very long time. He did not know it at the time. Ken had his travel agency decorated with clocks from different time zones around the world. They were all up on one wall. After that, the phone rang. Ken did not answer it. Customers who called never bought anything. They wasted Ken's time. Time was all that Ken had left. Ken did not even have any credit left. Ken only had three more checks left. He looked at his watch. It got 22 channels. It was almost time to go. Ken had to do something that day. It was a Friday. It made him angry. The phone stopped ringing. That made him glad. Ken had been experiencing sudden mood swings lately. They did not bother him that much. They bothered other people more. Ken had a family. Ken's deluxe black leather office chair had casters for easy mobility. Ken pushed himself back from his desk. He rolled on the chair mat. The hundreds of cleats on the underside of the chair mat gripped the carpet and kept the chair mat in place. It was summer. Ken poured himself a cup of coffee. Ken's coffee cup said Carnival Cruises on it. Carnival Cruises offered a wide array of quality cruises which presented outstanding value for the money. Ken said that to customers. The cup was white and the words on it were blue. Ken once took a 5-day Carnival Cruise to the Caribbean. He was accompanied by Shelly. Their stateroom had ample drawer and closet space. They spent a lot of time in their stateroom. Ken and Shelly walked along the City Light Boulevard at night. The sports deck was above the promenade deck. The top deck was the sun deck. Ken gave the cruise line an excellent rating. It was a business trip. Ken told his wife the weather was beautiful. He sent her a postcard. Ken was reminiscing. Then Ken finished his coffee. It smelled burnt. Ken took a piss and did not wash his hands. He left the toilet seat up. The fat, little Mexican lady did a wonderful job cleaning Ken's travel agency. She wiped up all the pubic hair. Ken was very content with her. He could never remember her name. Then Ken started to do what he had to do that day. Things were never the same after that. Even now Ken does not know how it all could have happened. Ken had to do what his wife asked him to do. She more or less told him to do it. It was supposed to only take Ken one hour. Ken's wife had her final exam that day. She was going to be a healing arts practitioner. Ken's wife had grown tired of retail. Ken's wife worked in women's fashion. She dressed in a fashionable manner. Ken secretly thought his wife still looked great for two kids. She was making him move out. He already found a condo that was in the area. It had a vaulted ceiling and a ceiling fan. Ken took his keys out of his pocket. Ken's wife was getting a new refrigerator delivered at 11:00 a.m. Ken had to be there for the delivery because Ken's wife could not be there. Ken's keys made a jingling noise. They were on a keychain. Ken locked up. He stood on the sidewalk in front of his travel agency and listened to the loudness of the jackhammer. They were widening the road. Ken was glad. He appreciated a wide road. Ken walked towards his car.

His shoes were called Graham. He bought them because he liked them way more than Ernest. It was not even close. Ernest was too pointed. Graham was a refined, casual shoe. Refined casuals were not just for Fridays anymore. Ken heard his name being called. Ken knew it was his name. Ken knew what his name was. He looked up. It was Shelly. She was right there. So was Ken. They both were. Ken and Shelly were in the middle of the parking lot. No cars were coming or anything. Shelly said hi. So did Ken. Shelly looked at Ken's face. Ken's eyes were red. His face was puffy. He needed a shave. Ken looked at all of Shelly. It was an opportunity for Ken to do so. Shelly asked Ken how things were going. Shelly was just being nice. Ken pictured Shelly in the shower. Ken told Shelly they were getting a new fridge delivered. He said it was going to be a side-by-side refrigerator this time. Shelly said she always wanted a side-by-side refrigerator. Ken told her what color it was going to be. Shelly said she liked that color. Ken asked Shelly if she wanted to come and see it. Shelly stuck her hand in her purse. Ken knew Shelly had Mace in her purse. She said no. Shelly said she had to go open up. She pulled out her keys. Shelly's keys were also on a keychain. Shelly did not want anything from Ken anymore. Ken did not totally feel the same way. There were several things he still would have wanted. He said bye. So did Shelly. Ken did not move. Shelly walked to her hair salon. She cut between a row of cars. Ken watched Shelly's body walk away. Ken liked the back of Shelly's body almost as much as the front. Together, they made Shelly who she was. He got into his car. Ken was driving the old one. The old car was a piece of shit. Ken's wife had the new car that day. It was a big day for Ken's wife that day. She was specializing in massage therapy as well as baths, wraps, and scrubs. Reflexology was considered a component of massage therapy. The Swedish massage was the most popular therapeutic massage. It was known throughout the world. It relaxed muscles and improved circulation. The deep tissue massage was only for the person who wanted deep work. Trigger point therapy was necessary for a deep tissue massage. The lymphatic cleanser was one of many detoxifying baths. It aided in the removal of toxins from the body. Ken knocked his head on the rearview mirror when he got in the car. Ken was mad even before he knocked his head. He started the car. It did not start. Then it did. It was hot in the car. Ken started to drive. Ken drove around the parking lot. He found Shelly's car. Her bumper sticker said, Honk if you wanna haircut. Ken's bumper sticker said something else. Ken pulled up next to Shelly's car. He adjusted the rearview mirror. Ken saw no one behind him. He spit a loogie on her fender. His window was open. Then Ken drove out of the parking lot and took a left. He drove slowly and cautiously because of the construction. Ken was not looking to get a traffic violation. His left arm was hanging out of the window. It was the loser arm. Ken's short-sleeve, button-down, polycotton navy shirt had equal amounts of comfort and style. Ken pulled his arm back in and put on the air. Ken cruised through a yellow light. It was not red. Ken kept his eyes on the road. He passed the nursing home. Every time Ken passed the nursing home, he had to think of his mom. She lived there. Ken drove straight home. Then he turned into his subdivision. Ken saw the delivery truck in his driveway. The delivery truck was already there. Ken parked at the curb and got out. The delivery man got out of his truck. He was young and fat. The delivery man had a round, pale face. A shiny wrench was sticking out of the front middle pocket of the delivery man's overalls. He was eating a Double Nut Neptune. Ken told him that that was his favorite candy bar. Ken apologized for being late. The delivery man told Ken not to sweat it. The delivery man said he just got there, too. He was a nice delivery man. The delivery man rode up the truck's automatic loading ramp. He rode back down with a dolly. Ken asked the delivery man if he needed any help. The delivery man said he did not need any help. He was already finished with his candy bar. The height of the dolly provided the leverage needed to move refrigerators, freezers, and washers. It had rub rails to protect from scratches and mars. The delivery man went into Ken's house. Dave came over. Ken and Dave had already said hi to each other when Ken got out of his car. Dave lived across the street from Ken. Dave was out shooting baskets. Dave's driveway was bigger and flatter than Ken's driveway. Dave had a three-point line painted on his driveway. He was an engineer. Dave asked Ken if their Wiffle ball game was still on for tomorrow. Ken said it was. Dave said he was glad to hear that. Dave told Ken he finally got his riser working. Dave had a batter's box taped on the back of his house. He used electrical tape. Ken asked Dave how he threw it. Dave said he threw it side arm with the holes down. He said he put his index and middle fingers above the holes along the seam and placed his thumb on the seam on the opposite side. He said he held his ring finger and pinky together at the center of the ball where the trademark and the patent number were. Ken said that he followed him. Dave said he was able to get it to rise between two and three feet because he had his whip motion down. Dave said that with his whip motion down Ken was not going to be able to touch his riser. Ken said bullshit. He said he was going to send Dave's riser up on the roof. Wiffle balls did not get stuck in their gutters because Ken and Dave both had gutter fencing. Gutter fencing was difficult to put up, but it was worth it in the long run. Ken and Dave both thought so. Ken and Dave were arch rivals as neighbors, but as a team they were in second place. They were the Crawdads. Dave said he would drop by tomorrow at their usual time. Then Dave swished one from his curb, did a reverse lay-up off the first bounce, and went inside. The delivery man came back out with the old fridge. He was very good with a dolly. The delivery man got the old fridge onto the loading ramp without difficulty. Ken stepped onto the loading ramp, too, and rode up the loading ramp with the delivery man. The delivery truck was 1538 cu. ft. Ken saw the new refrigerator. It was not in a box. Ken said he was surprised the refrigerator was not in a box. The delivery man said that they used foam now. They approached the refrigerator. Ken felt the truck's suspension under his feet. He rested one hand on the new refrigerator. Ken asked the delivery man if he could ask him something. The delivery man said that that was fine. Ken paused. He looked around at the convenient, padded rub rails on each of the truck's interior walls. Ken felt right at home. The delivery man wanted to know what Ken wanted to ask. Ken asked the delivery man if he would deliver the new refrigerator around to his back yard. The delivery man said he would as long as Ken would sign for it. Ken said he would, so the delivery man said he would. Ken said it had to do with his wife. Ken told the delivery man that he and his wife were having some marital problems. The delivery man said his parents got divorced back when he was in sixth grade. Ken patted the delivery man on the shoulder. Ken said thanks. The delivery man brought the refrigerator out to Ken's back yard. Ken said that he thought it would look nice next to the dogwood. The delivery man put it there. He asked Ken if he wanted him to remove the foam packaging. Ken said that would be great. Ken gave the delivery man a nice tip. The delivery man left. Ken stood in his back yard next to his refrigerator. From where he was standing, Ken could see Paul sitting on a lawn chair in his garage. Paul was cleaning his clubs. He was retired. Paul was not allowed to open the windows in his house because his wife said the drapes got dirty when the windows were open. Paul sat in his garage a lot. Ken waved to Paul, and Paul waved back. They went golfing together once a week. Ken was going to miss his friends when he moved. Ken flipped through the user's manual. It said the refrigerator was tan. Ken opened one of the doors. It was the freezer. There were slide-out wire freezer baskets in there for quick and easy access. Ken closed the freezer door and opened the other door. The refrigerator had crispers with automatic humidity control. One shelf rolled up and down to accommodate tall items. The manual said it was called the elevator shelf. There was an egg bin with a lid. Ken had always liked a good egg. He closed that door, too. Ken rolled up the user's manual and whacked himself on the leg with it. Ken went inside. He poured himself a drink. He needed to take a shower. Ken took a drink. The latest Pope John Paul II plate was hanging up on the wall. Ken's wife collected plates. It was the first plate Ken's wife hung up all by herself. Ken's wife said she could do things by herself. The kitchen looked so different without a refrigerator. Ken did not know what they could possibly have for dinner. Ken ate some peanuts with his drink. They were salted. High blood pressure was one way to die. Then Ken took a hot, wet shower. It felt good. He remembered the one time Shelly took a shower there. Ken was with her in the shower. Shelly only took a shower there once because they felt it was not the right thing to do. It was a great time. They did it in the shower. Shelly said she liked the way Ken's wife decorated the house. That was about all Ken remembered. Ken turned off the water. He was dripping wet. He stepped onto the amethyst butterfly bath rug. It was a definite crowd pleaser. Lovely sage green and lavender butterfly patches were embroidered on opposite corners. Ken grabbed a towel. He dried off with it. Ken heard voices. Voices were coming from the back yard. Ken peeked from behind the shade. He peeked because he was still naked. Ken was almost dry. Ken's family was down there in the back yard. Ken's two children were trying to walk on the grass in their in-line skates. Ken did not know which one was which because they had on their protective gear. They were boys. Ken's wife looked baffled. She was talking on the phone. Ken put on his blue bathrobe. He opened the window. He said hi to everyone. Everyone looked to see where Ken's voice was coming from. Ken said he was up in the master bath. Everyone looked up. Ken's boys were happy to see him. They started doing stunts for Ken. Ken said they were great ones. Ken told them just to watch out for the refrigerator. Ken's boys said they were watching out. Ken asked his wife how her final exam went. Ken's wife asked Ken what the new refrigerator was doing in the back yard. She was wearing the multi-stripe relaxed blouse she bought for the final exam. It was the epitome of subdued sophistication. Ken tightened the belt of his bathrobe. Ken did not want his private parts to show. Ken said he had no idea. He said he did not even know the new refrigerator had been delivered at all. Ken said he would be right down. Ken's wife said she was trying to reach somebody about the refrigerator. She said she was on hold. Ken asked his wife who she was trying to reach. Ken's wife said that she first tried the store. Ken asked his wife what the store said. Ken's wife said the store said they did not know anything about it. Then Ken's wife said she tried the delivery company. Ken asked her if they knew anything about it. Ken's wife said they kept transferring her all over and that now she was on hold. She said she almost did not have any talk time left. Ken said he would be right there. Ken had been holding the shower squeegee the whole time. Ken and his wife squeegeed the shower walls after every shower. They did not want the caulking to turn black or green. Ken said he just had to squeegee the shower and then he would be right there. Ken's wife hung up. She screamed. She was angry. She put her cell phone in her fashion-forward hemp tote. It displayed colorful hues and was earth-friendly. Ken's wife said her battery was out. She told Ken to bring his phone down when he came down. Ken said he would. He said he would be right down. He said he would squeegee the walls later. Ken closed the window. He walked through the house and down the deck steps to the back yard. He had clothes on now. His two boys started running towards him. He said they should take off their skates, but they did not want to. He gave them both a big bear hug at the same time. Ken suggested that they at least take off their protective gear. He said they must be hot. It was a hot day. Ken's boys said they were not hot. Ken was glad his children liked their protective gear so much. It saved lives. It was expensive, too. Ken said hi to his wife. He could smell her perfume.

It smelled like flowers. Ken rested his hand on her shoulder and then took his hand back. Ken's hand did not belong there anymore. Ken's wife asked Ken if he had his phone. Ken said he sure did. It was attached at his waist. He was wearing shorts. Ken's wife said the whole thing was ridiculous. Ken agreed. He said it was pretty funny. He said it was pretty weird. Ken's wife asked Ken for his phone. Ken said he would try giving them a call himself. Ken told his wife not to worry about it. Ken said he would put some pressure on those jerk-offs. Ken said he would take care of the matter. Ken's wife told the two boys to go inside and get cleaned up. The two boys moaned and started falling all over the lawn. They said they did not want to. They said they were playing kangaroo. Ken told his sons that they could play kangaroo for two more minutes. His sons said they wanted to play kangaroo for five more minutes. Ken said they could play kangaroo for three more minutes. Ken had never seen them play kangaroo before. He asked his wife if it was a new game they learned at school. Ken's wife told Ken to call the delivery company. Ken grabbed his cell phone. He asked his wife to finally tell him how her final exam went. He wanted to know if he could call her a healing arts practitioner. Ken's wife said she passed her final exam. She said she got an A on her final exam. Ken congratulated his wife. Ken asked his two sons if they had congratulated their mother. He told them that their mother was now a healing arts practitioner. His sons did not hear him because they were hopping over on the side of the house. Ken told them to be careful with the woodpile. Ken's wife showed Ken the number to call and told him to call. Ken started calling. Ken asked his wife if she was still going to the final exam party at the Healing Arts Institute. Ken's wife said she was. Ken asked his wife if she would like him to come along with her. Ken's wife said no. She said they had already discussed it a hundred times. Ken finished dialing. Ken got an automated voice recording. He was put on hold. Ken told his wife that he was on hold. Ken's wife told the two boys that the three minutes were up. She told them to hop upstairs and clean up. She told them to take off their skates and protective gear in the garage. Ken stepped away from his wife and acted like he was no longer on hold. He started talking. It was all one big bluff. The whole time he was listening to jazz-type music. He kind of liked it. He wondered why he never listened to jazz. He finished talking and hung up. He clipped his phone back on to his waist. Ken took a deep breath. He turned to face his wife. Ken's wife asked Ken what they said. Ken lied. Ken said they were going to look into it. Ken's wife wanted to know when they were going to take care of it. Ken said they said they would take care of it as soon as possible. Ken's wife wanted to know when that was. Ken said they said by tomorrow at the latest. Ken's wife wanted to know if they were supposed to leave the refrigerator outside until they took care of it. Ken said that was a good question. Ken's wife said she just could not believe it. Ken said he really could not believe it either. Ken told his wife that they would just have to stick together and get through it together. Ken's wife did not respond. Ken said he wanted to hear all about her exam. Ken's wife said she already told him. She said she said she got an A. Ken said congratulations. He said he knew she could do it. Ken's wife said she had to go get ready. Ken reached for his wife's hand. Ken's wife told Ken to let go. Ken let his wife's hand go. Ken's wife went inside. Ken stayed outside a second. He waved to Paul. Then Ken followed his wife into the house. Ken's wife kicked off her mules as she stepped into the house. They looked Italian. They were sleek and shiny. Their pointed toes were embellished with detailing. The boys were playing a video game. They said they were ready. They were twins. Ken asked his wife what they were ready for. Ken's wife said they were going to a slumber party. Ken said he had not been aware of that. Ken's wife said she forgot to tell him about it. Ken said he thought he was going to have some quality time with his sons. Ken's wife said he would have the rest of the weekend. Ken and his wife reached the top of the stairs. Ken was still walking behind his wife. Ken said he had been thinking. Ken's wife said she was going to take a shower. Ken knew that meant he had to wait outside. Ken said he could tell her what he had been thinking when she got out. Ken's wife closed the door. Ken sat on the stairs and waited for his wife to take a shower. Ken heard John Madden's voice coming from the boys' video game. It was football. John Madden's voice brought back memories. Ken's wife came out. Her shoulders were bare. She had on a tube dress with smocked bust and ruffled trim. Ken stood up. His wife looked awesome. Ken said that if she had a second, he could tell her what he had been thinking. Ken's wife said she was in a hurry, but that she had a second. Her toenails were painted. Ken fiddled with a switch on the wall, and the attic fan turned on. It made a loud rumbling noise. Ken apologized. He turned it off. Ken said that with everything going on. He said by everything he meant the refrigerator. Ken said that it maybe was not the right time for him to be moving out. Ken said he thought maybe he should stay until things normalized. He said he was ready to normalize. Ken's wife did not agree. Ken's wife called downstairs to the boys. She said they should turn off their game and put their shoes on. She asked them if they had their sleeping bags, their PJs, and their toothbrushes. They said they had them. Ken's wife told Ken that if she did not come home tonight, she would pick up the boys tomorrow morning on her way home. She looked at herself in the hall mirror one more time. Then she went downstairs. Ken followed her downstairs. Ken stared at his wife's collar bone. Ken told his boys to have a great time. He gave them a thumbs-up. His boys said they would. Ken told them not to stay up too late. His boys said they were going to try to stay up all night. Then Ken's wife and two boys left. Ken was alone. He was going to have to get used to that feeling. Ken started to go to the fridge for a beer. Ken was so used to having a fridge. Everything was changing. Ken grabbed a beer from under the bar. He held it in his hand and stared into the family room. It made Ken glad to know that his boys liked their football video game so much. Ken went out onto the deck. He sat down on the chaise lounge. Ken stretched out on it. He enjoyed the timeless tradition of relaxing outdoors on it. Paul's garage door was down. That meant Paul was inside for the night. Ken opened his beer. He took a big gulp. After the big gulp, he put the can up on the left-hand work surface of his gas grill. There was not a slab of meat in the house. Ken adjusted his chaise lounge. It adjusted to four different positions. Ken picked the one he liked best. Ken put his hands behind his head. He drank his beer. He had bare feet. It was turning into a nice evening. Ken looked at the refrigerator in his back yard. It was an odd sight. Ken got another beer. Ken set up the oscillating sprinkler in the back yard. He was careful not to get the refrigerator wet. His medium ultimate deep dish with pepperoni and onion arrived. Ken ate a lot of it. Ken had to readjust his chaise lounge to eat it. Some cheese got on his t-shirt. It was pizza. Ken got another beer. The cans were lined up next to each other on the work surface. The sky was turning a darker shade of blue. Ken's oscillating sprinkler was still watering the same patch of lawn. Ken turned the stainless steel condiment basket over and over in his hands. It was empty. Ken filled the basket up with condiments when he barbequed. Ken used a lot of condiments. He liked them a lot. Ken stared through the holes of the condiment basket and recalled some of the memorable meals he had made at the grill. Ken knew that the flavorizer bars were the whole secret. Ken was glad he went with the grill with the flavorizer bars. Ken almost stepped in the last piece of pizza. Ken decided not to have another beer. He went into the garage and opened the utility bench. Ken took out his work boots. Heavy-duty work socks with double toe- and heel-stitching were stuffed in his work boots. Ken put them on first. Ken laced up his boots. Rakes, pruning tools, a post hole digger, edgers, and shovels were hanging up along one wall of the garage. Ken took down the shovel with the patented Power Collar. The durable textured powder coating on the tool head kept debris from sticking. Ken took it with him back to his back yard. He turned off the faucet. Ken walked over to the area he had been watering. His boots made squishy noises in the area. The area was wet. Ken pushed over the refrigerator. It landed with a loud crash. Then Ken started to dig. The first twenty minutes were easier than Ken thought they were going to be. Then Ken got a blister on his thumb and his back started to hurt. Ken put on garden gloves. He took off his shirt. Then Ken dug some more. Then Ken took a break. He sat down on the refrigerator. A mosquito flew up and bit him on the forehead. Ken went back to the garage and got out the Conceal candles. Conceal candles were better than Citronella and DEET because they were inhibitors. They made it difficult for mosquitoes to smell human targets. Ken was a human target. He lit three of them and placed them on the refrigerator. Ken started to dig again. Ken went up on the deck and ate the last piece of pizza. He was glad he did not step on it earlier. Ken liked cold pizza almost as much as hot pizza. Ken ate the piece of pizza with his garden gloves on. He walked back down into the yard. Ken shoveled some more. The lights were on in homes all around his neighborhood. They were Ken's neighbors. Ken did not have any garden torches to set up. They would have looked nice. Ken's hole was already knee-deep. He sat down again on the refrigerator. Ken was very careful not to sit down on the candles. They were working. Ken only had that one mosquito bite. Ken was too tired to stand back up. He lay down on his back. Ken looked up at the sky. The street lights made it too bright to see any stars. Ken closed his eyes. A June bug or some other kind of bug woke Ken up. Ken felt invigorated for a short period of time. He worked on his hole. Then Ken dropped the shovel and went inside. He got another beer. He flopped on the couch. He turned on the TV. The audience was laughing. Ken fell asleep. Ken woke up. The quaint, heritage pendulum wall clock over the mantelpiece was chiming. It had

Roman numerals. It was 7 a.m. The family room was bright. Cartoons were on. Ken watched one. He still had his boots on. The couch was dirty. Ken saw his footprints on the carpet. His wife was not going to like that. He walked to the pantry. It was hard for Ken to walk because his muscles hurt. Ken finished a bag of bite-size cookies with big chocolate chips. He made lemonade flavor drink. He did not overfill or mound the measuring cap when he made it. Ken made four servings. To retain freshness, Ken closed the mix container back up. He drank two servings right away. Ken ate the last banana in the fruit bowl. It looked like Pope John Paul II was looking right at him. Ken threw away the banana peel. It was garbage day. Ken wheeled the garbage can down to the curb. Ken looked at his neighbors' curbs to see if it was recycling day, too. It was. Ken walked back to his garage. Ken pulled out the bottom bin of the recycling tower. It was over three feet tall. It put a stop to recycling sprawl. The bottom bin was for aluminum. Ken carried the bottom bin down to the curb. He went around to the back yard. Ken put on his gloves. He picked up his shovel. Ken still had a lot more work ahead of him if he was going to bury the refrigerator. Paul's garage door opened up. They waved. Paul sat down and washed his golf balls. Ken made the hole a little wider. He went over next to the deck and took a leak. It was all the lemonade flavor drink he drank. Ken was having difficulties making the hole deeper. It was already pretty hot. Ken put the sprinkler on the hole to soften up the dirt more. It helped a little. It turned the dirt to mud. Ken got wet. It felt good. Ken was muddy. Little by little the hole was getting a little deeper. Dave came around back. Dave was wearing khaki slacks. A yellow polo went with it. Dave said he tried the doorbell but nobody answered. Ken said he was the only one home. He was standing down in the hole. It made Dave look even taller than he really was. Dave was taller than Ken. He had better posture. Dave asked Ken what he was doing. Ken stuck the shovel in the mud. He said he was burying their old refrigerator.

Dave asked Ken why he did not just have it hauled away the day before. Ken said it was going to cost him $45. Ken said he thought that was too much. Dave agreed. Dave asked Ken if he wanted him to turn off the sprinkler. Ken said not to worry about it. Dave said he had some bad news. Ken asked Dave what was up. Dave said his wife's father unexpectedly died last night. Ken said he was sorry to hear that. Dave said thanks. Ken told Dave to tell his wife he was sorry. Dave said he would tell her. Dave said they got the call in the middle of the night. He said they were packing up the car now and were leaving in a few minutes. Dave said he was going to have to cancel their Wiffle ball game today. Ken said that was okay. Ken said with all the digging. Dave asked Ken if he could get their mail for them while they were gone. Ken said no prob. Dave said he was flying back at the end of next week. He said his wife was going to stay a little longer. Dave said his wife's mother was probably going to come live with them. Dave said there were a lot of big changes on the horizon. Ken agreed to that. Then Dave said he had to go. Ken told Dave to drive safely. Dave said he would. He said they would play ball next weekend. Ken said that he probably could not play Wiffle ball next weekend. Dave wanted to know why. Ken said he probably could not play because he was moving out next weekend. Dave wanted to know what Ken meant by moving out. Ken flung some mud over his shoulder and said that him and his wife were getting a divorce. Dave said whoah. He asked Ken if him and his wife were really getting a divorce. Ken said they were. Ken said he was moving into the condos down by the Noah's Ark Motor Inn. Dave said he had heard of those places. He said he heard they were supposed to be nice. Dave said he was real sorry. He told Ken he would help him move if he needed any help. Ken said thanks. Then Dave had to go and left. Ken dug for about another hour. He did not have his watch on. The hole got a little deeper. The water bill was going to be through the roof. Ken's wife and his two boys appeared on the deck. Ken's wife screamed.

Ken's wife asked Ken what in the hell he was doing. The way she asked him made him a little mad. It was her tone of voice. Ken asked his wife what in the hell it looked like he was doing. Ken's two sons thought it was cool. They wanted to go down and play in the mud with their dad. Ken told them to come on down and play. Ken's wife would not let them. Ken's wife told them to stay up on the deck. Ken asked his sons how late they stayed up. They said they stayed up until three in the morning. Ken said that was pretty late. He asked them if they had a good time. They said they had a great time. Ken said that that was the most important thing. Ken told them that whatever they did, they should always try to enjoy life. Ken's wife told Ken to stop what he was doing. Ken told his wife that he was not going to stop now that he was almost done. Then Ken's wife put her hands on the deck railing and asked Ken if he was the one who put the refrigerator in the back yard in the first place. Ken said duh. He said it took her long enough to figure that one out. Ken's wife told the boys to get inside. First the boys did not move. Then they stepped into the kitchen. The deck was right off the kitchen. Ken's wife told Ken that she was calling the police. Ken asked his wife what she was going to tell them. She told Ken that she was going to tell them that her husband was destroying the house. Ken's sons were back out on the deck. Ken's wife told them to get back inside. They went back inside. Ken resumed his digging. The police came. They looked pretty relaxed about it. They walked around back. Paul stood up from his lawn chair, then he sat back down. Ken said hi to the police officers from down in the hole. He did not stop digging. The two policemen wanted to know what the problem was. Ken said he did not feel there was a problem. Ken said it was his back yard, his refrigerator, and his shovel. Ken's wife started yelling. The policemen told her to keep it down. Ken told the policemen that his wife flew off the handle a lot. The policemen asked Ken to step out of the hole. Ken said that he would be right out. He said that he was almost finished. The policemen said that he could finish it later. One of the policemen turned off the sprinkler. Ken asked him to turn it back on. The policeman did not turn the water back on. Ken told the policeman to turn his fucking water back on. The other policeman called in for back-up. Ken's wife started screaming again. Ken's wife said her husband was out of control. Ken said to his wife that she was the one who was screaming. The policemen told both of them to settle down. Ken said he was settled down. Ken said he was not the one with the problem. One policeman put his boot up on the refrigerator. He told Ken that he would be saving himself a lot of problems if he would just put down the shovel and climb out of the hole. Ken stopped digging. He looked up to the deck. His sons were kneeling down on the deck. They were looking at him between the spindles. They were his own flesh and blood. The policeman told Ken to put down the shovel and slowly get out of the hole. Ken got out of the hole. The policeman told Ken to drop his shovel. Ken held onto his shovel. He gripped the shovel with both hands. The second squad car arrived. Ken's wife screamed at the boys to get in the house. Ken told his wife to never ever scream at his sons like that again. Paul was standing in his garage. He had a wet rag in one hand and a golf ball in the other. He was wondering what was going on. The four policemen surrounded Ken. Ken told them to stay away. He held his shovel like a bat. The four policemen took a step forward. Ken took a swing. The policemen all took a step back. Ken told the four policemen to arrest his wife. One policeman told Ken that to their knowledge his wife had not done anything. Ken said his wife was kidnapping his two children from him. He said she was never going to let him see them again. Ken's wife screamed that that was not true. Ken told the policemen not to believe her. Ken said she was kicking him out of the house and taking his children. One policeman told Ken that nobody was taking anybody's children. Ken told him that he did not know dick about fuck. Ken's two sons were back out on the deck again. The policemen told Ken that the sooner he came with them, the sooner the problem would be rectified. Ken took another swing. The shovel slipped out of Ken's hands. It flew through the air. It hit one of the policemen on the arm. Ken's wife screamed. Ken said shit. The other policemen overpowered Ken. Ken was lying on his stomach before he knew it. Ken's hands were cuffed behind his back. Ken said he was really sorry. He said he did not mean to do that. He asked if the one policeman was hurt. The policemen did not respond. Ken had to remain on his stomach. He could see up to the deck. His two sons were crying. That made Ken cry, too. Everything hit him right then and there. They were saying not to hurt their dad. One policeman called in. The other policemen got Ken to his feet. Ken was dirty and exhausted. Tears were running down his cheeks. The policemen started to escort Ken to their cruiser. Ken looked at his two sons. Ken said, "Love ya, guys."

Tammy

Don was always pooped and fatigued. Don always felt restless. Restless leg syndrome always made it difficult for Don to stay asleep. It always woke him up. It made him lie there in the guest room and think about faraway places. It made him go to the kitchen and just sit there after he turned on the light over the stove. It is a common neurological disorder. There are over eighty known sleeping disorders. Don seemed to have had this one. Don frequently had unpleasant sensations in his legs. He frequently had an urge to move them for relief and to pack his car and move to a small town far away. Don said the feeling was like a tingling, a pulling, or even a crawling or wormy. The last two feelings are difficult to comprehend. Restless leg syndrome can influence occupational performance, social activities, and family life. Don's Sequoia chukkas have a padded collar for extra comfort. They have a mesh lining which allowed his feet to breathe. The rubber soles are flexible, slip resistant, and just inches above the ground. His wife is at home where she always is. Her name has not been decided yet. Tammy is the only other person in the store. Outlet shoes do not move well on Monday mornings. They move great on Saturdays. They move good on Fridays. They start to move better again on Tuesdays. She is standing at the door which she locked. Tammy works there. She is fiddling with a loose button on her heavy cream Henley. It has a ribbed knit. Its modern tunic style stretches over her rump which is large, but not too big. It can turn a lonely head. The lights are already on over at Wallpaper World. They are long tubes of bright fluorescent light which hum and shed light on thousands of available wallpaper and border patterns. Tammy likes going to Wallpaper World on her lunch hour. She sees Rob's car. Rob can be hilarious. He introduced her to wallies. Wallies are wallpaper cutouts that stick on the wall like stickers. Fish wallies are big sellers around bathroom fixtures. He showed her them. They were colorful, smiling fish. Tammy liked them, but wanted a different kind of a wallie so Rob showed her different wallies. Tammy selected a moose wallie because of her aunt who lives way up in Canada. That is something unique about Tammy. Tammy's girlfriends only have relatives who live right here in town. It is a city for all seasons. Places of interest included the outlet center, Hunan Chinese Rest, El Jimador, and the Waffle House. One girlfriend has cousins who live across the state line. The wallies look real as they walk in front of tall pine trees which also look real. They were real easy to stick on. Rob said they would be. He made this lewd joke about their dewlaps. That made Tammy laugh and call Rob gross. Rob licked his finger and poked it up in the air and let it sizzle there. Tammy wants to know when Rob is ever going to ask her out to Friday's. His bumper sticker says that he is divorced and loving it. She uses 2000 Flushes. It makes flushing funner. It turns the water blue and will not harm pets or children. Returning now to the scene of the crime, or at least the scene. It may not have been a crime. The police are on their way and will decide that. The outlet shoe store is located next to the American Tourister. They have suitcases, carry-ons, garment bags, duffels and more. Don and Linda will no longer be able to travel. They only tried it again once after their son died about three years after he died. They went to the Ozarks in the off-season. The Ozarks is a nice, relaxing placid place that offers speed boat rentals and where you can test your aim at a shooting gallery in one of the many arcades. It drizzled the whole time and was cold. You could tell right away it was the off-season. Linda stayed in their room the whole time. Don finally left the room. He tried ice-skating. He went around and around with one hand close to the railing. There was no music playing. The only other one there was the little girl prodigy who is always there and in the local papers and her trainer who have their eyes set on 2016. Don's ankles started to hurt, and he went back. Linda was still sitting in the exact same spot when he got back. Linda can stare into space for hours or months, imagining her son's fatal car crash. Their hotel room was done in warm, inviting tones. The tones were burgundy and hunter green and overlooked their car and the pool which was drained for the winter. Don massaged his feet. He put on a second pair of socks. He sat on the bed. They watched Ghostbusters that night and packed and left the next morning. They did not forget anything under the bed or in the closet because Don double-checked. Business has always been steady, if not great. Don even carried bowling shoes because of the bowling alley down the road. He had business acumen. They are located at the end of aisle 3. That is down where the office is and where Don is hanging. He also stocked various leather items such as belts and wallets. They may be found up by the cash register. Shoplifting is a problem even in this small town of seven thousand. One of Tammy's jobs is to hang articles on the display racks which teeter and squeak when customers revolve them. The rack with the men's athletic crew, low cut, and quarter socks is tipped over. It came down with a crash. It got in Don's way and bought Tammy a little time. She faked right and cut left down women's. She did not stop until she got past Animal Instincts, the brand made of real leather. They are hot items. Tammy has been in sales in one form or other ever since high school. Tammy never made the grade as hostess. She never had braces. Then after the manager torched Ponderosa, Tammy worked at the batting cages and go-kart track. She made change. She had lots of time to talk on the phone and paint her nails different dark colors. Her and her friends smoked pot out there at night, sitting on the tires which lined the go-kart track and smoking pot. Somebody's hand was always trying to get down her pants. She always had nice pants. Then when that place got sold and developed, Tammy got her big break in retail and eventually had an abortion and matured. She got rid of her curls. Don knew she would do well and blossom in outlet shoes. Don sometimes looked at pictures when he was alone, and sometimes he painted his own pictures. They were pictures where long, straight roads converged on the horizon. He wanted to show her them. Tammy said okay and found their house easy. Their house was the only house that had a ramp leading up to the front door of the house. Tammy had never talked to someone in a wheel chair before that night. It made her want to bend over. It surprised her how low down Linda looked. Linda said it was her hip, but Don said it was her mind and made these wide, scary eyes. It was supposed to be for dinner. Don got Tammy downstairs and to see his pictures. He was not a professional painter, but his perspective looked good. The roads all got narrower and narrower, and Don kept getting in her space. She smelled his aftershave. Don's hand knocked twice against Tammy's hand, so she put it in her pocket. It was a little like today when all of a sudden his face got all in Tammy's face and neck and at first she did not know what was going on. Then Tammy was like, don't fucking tell me. Then Linda wanted to show Tammy Donny's room, and they still had not eaten yet. Tammy's stomach was growling the whole time. Tammy could smell the roast and potatoes all the way from Donny's room. Linda told Tammy not to sit down on Donny's bed. That creeped Tammy out. Donny was on his way back from college for a visit, and like all college kids, the roads were wet and he was exceeding the speed limit. Donny was the first one in both their families to ever go to college. He was smart. Linda showed Tammy the college sweatshirt that his friends from his engineering class gave them at his funeral. Everybody hugged everybody. Linda stopped talking, and Tammy could tell Linda had transported herself back to then and the past. Then Linda said that afterwards life just went on for everybody else. She sounded all bitter about it. Tammy wondered what else they were supposed to do, like all drive into a pylon or something? Tammy was starving. She was glad when the oven started buzzing. Then Linda said the f-word. Tammy could not believe it. She said the f-word, got up out of her wheel chair and went to turn off the buzzer. Tammy thought about snooping around the room some. The meat was tender and juicy, and there was plenty of potatoes. Dessert was a giant cookie. It had to be at least half an inch thick. They gave her this big piece and then just sat there watching her eat it. Once Tammy finished it and put her fork down and wiped her mouth, she said she had to go. Tammy did not like it at Don and Linda's. Tammy could tell they wanted her to stay more because they asked her to. Then Don and Linda showed Tammy to the door and then stood there in the doorway the whole time while Tammy fumbled for her keys and got in and prayed her car would finally start, a problem her car has been having lately. The engine cranks in a repetitive-sounding pattern. Tammy has a bad timing chain or belt, but car repairs cost an arm and a leg. Linda was back in her wheelchair. Don and Linda looked forlorn just standing and sitting there in the doorway. The CD picked up where it left off on Hey Wait a Minute. Tammy almost plowed their mailbox. It is probably too late now to try and get tickets for REO's Time to Fly tour. Tammy had off the next day. The next day Tammy did not have off and had to go to work and went, she got there and found a small gift bag hanging where she usually hangs up her coat or jacket and her hobo named Carla or her clutch Lucia. It is Carla Tammy is now digging through to find some identification. The police want to see some, who have arrived. They parked right in the no-parking zone right in front. They are the authorities. Tammy tells them she was not surprised to see the small gift bag hanging there because it did not even occur to her that it was for her. So at first she saw it, but it did not register type thing, if they knew what she meant. The lady cop nods and asks Carla to continue about the gift bag. And if she can describe the contents of the gift bag, which Carla goes on to. The other cop goes and finds Don up in the back room. The belt he used is from his own store. It has a silver griffin buckle. Carla says the bag was from Bath & Body Works and was a red bag. She says she did not even think to look inside until Don asked her if she had looked inside. It was a tube of Sövage Instant Lip Plumper. Carla says she said thanks and how that maybe she would sell more shoes that way. Like how when waitresses wear low-cut things so their boobs half hang out so they get more tips. The cop wants to know when that was. Carla says it all just happened last week. Then the cop asks her if she ever applied the cream. Carla says uh-huh. She says but that it did not do her any good because her lips are so thin and chapped, and that there is no way a little cream is ever going to make a crud of difference. The cop asks if any other gifts followed, and Carla responds. Then she says that then this whole freaky thing today of him coming on to her like when she was back in high school. The cop asks Carla if her Henley was torn as a result, and Carla answers that question, too. She says the next thing she knew or heard was this gurgling sound from the back. The way the other cop, who is back, looks and nods at the other cop, makes it seem like he is confirming that that is probably what happened. The other cop looks at Carla's license some more and says Bane?, and that the street rings a bell, but she cannot place it. Carla says it is over by Greg's Auto Body. This time both cops nod. They know all about Greg. Greg's garage is right across from Carla's apartment building. Her efficiency is up on the fourth floor. When Carla stands and looks out the window, she can see far. She can see the water tower, which is tall and big and round at the top. She can also see down on the other roofs. One has lawn furniture and a little grill up there. Guys from Water & Sewer go up there and have parties up there. They barf and wag their dicks in the air, depending on what the weather is like.

Horns Overflowing

Walter asks Joan to pass the salt ball grinder. Walter and Joan are married. It is early afternoon. Walter has already helped himself to the stuffing. Joan just sat down. Walter sat down before she did. Joan drove all the way to see Brad and back this morning. Joan had to leave really early. It was still dark out. It is a long drive there and back. She hopes Walter likes the stuffing. She was not so sure about the raisins. Joan tried a new recipe this year. The stuffing has onions, celery, wild rice, pecans, poultry seasonings, and raisins in it. Joan almost left the raisins out. She followed the magazine's make-ahead tip and refrigerated the vegetables and nuts two days before. It saved Joan time, and her refrigerator has the space. Joan and Walter are sitting at the dining room table. They can look right at each other if they want to. The one-handed operation of the large mill makes freshly ground salt readily available. Joan believes freshly ground salt makes a difference. Joan believes a lot of things. She believes her son will resume a normal life once he gets out. Walter is different. The pepper ball grinder is on the table, too. Joan set the table last night. Joan wanted the table to look perfect. The table looks nice. There are a lot of nice things on the table. Joan bought the ball grinders as a set. Walter uses his own peppermill. Walter's peppermill is right next to his 20-ounce crystal goblet which catches the light beautifully. The goblets have to be washed by hand. Walter washes them by hand because Joan always breaks them when she washes them by hand.

They once made love in their basement against a support pole. It was a long time ago. Their feelings for one another have since changed. The support poles are attached to I-beams running the length of the house. The support poles and the I-beams really keep the house up. Walter started demolishing Brad's beer can collection in the basement towards the end of summer. It is fall now. Walter enjoys spending time alone in the basement. Joan does not go down there. Joan and Walter used to like the same program with the funny black man. They used to laugh at the same funny jokes. The dish liquid and antibacterial hand soap with power sudsing that Walter uses to wash the goblets gives him a whole new level of dishwashing performance. Walter looks out the window over the sink when he washes dishes at the kitchen sink. He tries to see things that are not there. Walter bought his pepper pump not long after Joan bought the salt and pepper ball grinders. The pepper pump is an essential at the table and in the kitchen. Walter never wanted the ball grinders. He only needs to push the plunger on the top to grind the pepper. Joan bought the ball grinders because the crank on their Towne Oak peppermill was not working properly. The crank was wobbly. Joan thought it was something they could talk about. It was a warm day that day. A nice warm breeze was coming in through the windows. Joan was standing at their kitchen island. They have a kitchen butcher block work island. Joan started to mention the crank and how that it was wobbly. It was going to be a conversation. Walter drifted in and back out of the kitchen. Joan prefers when Walter is out of the house. Joan envisions many things that would be nice but that never happen. That makes Joan sad. Joan has a lot of feelings inside. Some of Joan's feelings are about Walter. Walter's goal is to care less and less about everything. Walter finds it hard to believe that he was once a dentist. Joan passes Walter the salt ball grinder. The table measures 44" x 72". With two aproned leaves it can open to 112". Walter squeezes the salt ball's ergonomic handle. Salt comes out. Joan folds her hands. She wants to pray. Joan says the prayer to herself. Joan does not want Walter to hear what she is praying for. Joan sometimes prays for Walter to die. The prayer just comes out that way. It makes Joan feel bad. Walter picks up his fruit napkin ring. It accentuates the table. It is reminiscent of nature's abundance at harvest. Joan loves to coordinate napkin rings with time. Walter looks through his napkin ring. He can see all of Joan's head through his napkin ring. Her eyes are closed. Joan is praying again. Walter is now able to look at Joan without feeling a single thing. He looks out the window. There is a big tree in the front yard. Brad helped Walter plant it. It was small when they planted it. Now it is taller than the house. It was a long time ago. The leaves are falling off the tree. Walter will blow them tomorrow. Leaf Magik has a 230 MPH blow speed and an anti-clog system. Joan makes the sign of the cross. Joan thinks she prayed for the right things today. Leaf Magik goes from blower to mulcher at the press of a button. It is time to eat. There is a lot of food on the table. In comparison with butter or oil, no-stick cooking spray adds only a trivial amount of fat and calories. Joan does not like her thighs. Women usually do not. Men like thighs the more they are spread. In his prime, Walter had a handicap of 2. Joan read that no-stick cooking spray can also be sprayed directly on the turkey for better browning. Joan is always on the look-out for new ideas. Joan is a small-business owner. Joan says she thinks the turkey looks browner this year. Walter does not know if the turkey looks browner. Walter is mentally beyond all colors. The apron Walter has to wear at work is green. He is wearing it now. Walter has a job again. He is a bagger. Walter has to go in to work after they eat. He is a bagger. Walter's bowtie is green, too. As a dentist, he used to wear a white coat at work. It is ironic. Joan asks Walter if he would like to cut the bird. Walter says he would. Walter pushes back his chair and stands up. Walter and Joan have Saxony cut pile carpet in their dining room. It is stain-resistant. Walter bends over towards the turkey. He is careful not to bump his head on the chandelier. The turkey is on an ovenproof pheasant platter right under the chandelier. There are two pheasants pictured on the platter. One pheasant is in front of the other pheasant. Both pheasants are brown, but they are looking off in different directions. Their heads are turned different ways. Tiers of translucent beads with suspended, teardrop-shaped ornaments drape like garlands from the chandelier. Walter does not bump his head. He has been ducking under the chandelier for longer than he cares to remember. He turns on his cordless electric knife. It takes two hours to fully charge. The handle is designed for right- and left-handed people. Walter is right-handed. Joan is right-handed, too. Their son and daughter are also right-handed. His name is Brad, and her name is Claire. Claire is older. Brad and Claire will not be coming to dinner. Brad is in a minimum security prison. He is allowed to wear his own clothing. Walter knows some people who are left-handed. Joan does not know if she knows anybody who is left-handed. It is a 13-pound turkey. Walter carves it. He still has moments when he would like to cut his house apart. The property value in their subdivision continues to rise. Walter has always invested wisely in mutual funds. Walter and Joan's house is made of studs, plasterboard, vinyl siding, and other material. The cordless electric knife will cut up to 45 minutes of bread or meat. Walter is 57. Joan is not. Her French-style napkin with the cheerful yellow background is in her lap. The crackled appearance makes it look traditional. The tablecloth is highlighted with the same lovely blue design. The tablecloth takes a long time to iron because it is 100% cotton. Joan does not mind ironing because ironing is something to do when she is home. She has a new iron. The two-way Steam Clean system will prolong the life of Joan's iron by flushing out lint and minerals while continuously cleaning the steam valve. Joan holds out her plate for Walter. Walter places a piece of meat on Joan's plate where the stunning floral motif is. The plate has a gold band around it. Joan says it looks delicious. Walter's plate looks exactly like Joan's plate. He puts some meat on it. Joan slices open a sweet potato with her knife. The stainless steel flatware is both lustrous and strikingly simple. It is named after a southern French town. There is a bee on each bolster. Joan likes things with bees on them. Joan's favorite sweater has a bumble bee on it. Joan pours goldenrod honey on her sweet potato. Goldenrod is a well-known fall composite. It covers old fields, pastures, and the open woods throughout North America. Joan says that goldenrod honey is a dependable honey. Joan pushes goldenrod honey when a customer is not interested in a more exotic or expensive variety of honey. Joan has a honey stand in the mall's west wing. She stocks over sixty distinct types of honey on her little yellow cart. Her little cart is cute. She has honey ranging from water white to dark brown, from acacia to wildflower. Joan's business is called Honey Bee Good. Honey Bee Good was even featured in the local paper. People like Honey Bee Good. She wears her favorite sweater to work a lot. People like it. Walter sits back down. Walter's chair has armrests. Walter rests them there for a moment. There is a spot on the wall he always thinks is a bug. Joan puts a piece of cornbread on her plate. Walter puts some things on his plate. He tries a baby carrot with glazed brown sugar. Joan raises her wine glass. She says they forgot about the wine. Joan's wine charm is a cheese charm. Walter's wine charm is a grape charm. Joan is always the cheese charm. That way they never confuse who has which glass. Walter reaches over to the sideboard. He pulls a bottle of wine from the wine sling made of handcrafted Nambé metal. It will not crack or chip. Walter's foil cutter leaves a neat edge for pouring. He has an ultimate cork pulling machine. Walter pours the wine. Walter and Joan say cheers. They always have. The wine's bouquet goes well with the meal's flavor. There is a wall sconce with mirror on the wall. Nothing comes to anyone's mind. Joan eats a lot. Walter takes a bite. Joan says she is having her two Meghans help her out tomorrow since they are off of school tomorrow. The Meghans are best friends. They have the same first name. They are on the varsity spirit squad. Claire is flying out east for the four-day weekend. Claire said she would call today. The day after Thanksgiving is the biggest day of the year in retail. The mall opens at 6 a. m. One day Joan wants to have her own store at the mall. The self-help group Joan attends encourages her to have her own store. They tell her to go for it. Joan asks Walter if he went golfing today. He says he did. He says it was windy. Joan asks if he was still able to clear the water on the fourth hole. Walter says he was because the wind was at his back. He says his ball sailed right over the creek. Walter's gray-and-charcoal golf bag has six zip-up pockets and a water ball retriever holder. Walter now uses his golf clubs to smash Brad's beer cans. He never golfs anymore. Sometimes he just stomps on the beer cans. Walter destroys Brad's beer can collection when Joan is at work. Joan once gave Walter a golf ball monogrammer. Joan switches her fork to her right hand and tells Walter that Brad said to say hi. The china cabinet in Walter and Joan's dining room has a lighted interior with dimmer. A hammered copper bowl from Claire is on one of the shelves. She teaches anthropology at a small college. The white, roomy, earthenware tureen for presenting soups was made in Italy. It is the biggest item in the whole china cabinet. It has a 15-cup capacity. The lantern to the left mimics the style of island bamboo. There are four gold mosaic votive holders on the bottom shelf. Joan likes the way candles burn. Joan stores the Christmas dinnerware down in the cabinets below. Walter and Joan's china cabinet is big and heavy. Joan says she has good news. She says Brad found out that he is going to be able to pursue the law degree online. Walter takes the lid off the attractive and functional butter crock. Walter is going to have a roll. The butter has not been shaped into a duck or other farm animal. It looks like the tip of an iceberg. Walter uses the butter knife lying next to the butter crock. The rolls are still warm. Walter loves the delicious taste of freshly baked rolls with a minimum of effort. He likes how the

Bakery Boon has a crust control. It is a dial. He can watch the baking process through the large viewing window. Walter spreads butter onto his roll. Walter replaces the lid on the butter crock and takes a bite of his roll. Joan tells Walter that Brad told her that he is going to make it. Then Joan turns her head away from the table. She still gets choked up about Brad. Joan is facing the Ansel Adams picture. It is called Snake River. The river looks like a snake. Walter often wanders through the house during the day. When he stops in front of the picture, he runs his finger down the river in search of a drowning man. Walter tells Joan he will be bagging alongside Big Al tonight. Big Al is over 70. He loves to whistle old songs. He loves old songs. Walter has four different ways of asking the customers if they would like paper or plastic. There are some basic rules for bagging. Never overload is one. Frozen items always go in plastic is another rule. Walter is allowed to wear comfortable shoes. A phone rings. Walter takes his phone out of his apron pocket. Walter says it is Rex. Walter has two numbers saved on his cell phone. Rex is the supermarket manager. He wears a whistle around his neck like a coach. Joan checks to make sure her phone is on. She hopes nothing has happened to Claire. She does not know why Claire has not called yet. It is even later on the east coast. Walter says hi to Rex. He tells Rex he was just thinking about him. Walter says he is ready to bag. Walter listens to what Rex says. Then Walter says that he will come in anyway. He says he needs to work off some of the bird. Walter pats his stomach. Walter tells Rex that Joan cooked an absolutely delicious meal. Joan puts her phone back on the buffet next to the hand-molded ceramic rooster. The rooster is stunningly detailed. Joan bought it at a winery. Joan still regrets that she did not buy the hen to go with it. The irresistible hen was the perfect mate for the strutting rooster. Walter tells Rex not to worry about it. He says he really wants to come in. He says he can tell his wife wants to talk about their son again. Walter asks Rex if he ever told him he even had a son. Rex answers. Walter asks him if he remembers the story about the frat-house rape. Joan gets a sick look on her face. Walter tells Rex it was in all the papers. Joan gets up from the table. Her chair tips back against the buffet, and her napkin falls to the floor. Joan does not pick it up. Joan leaves the room. She goes into the kitchen. The kitchen has both a pantry and a closet. Joan keeps things like the vacuum and the ironing board in the closet. Joan really wants a new bagless vacuum. The Root 6 Cyclone does not lose suction over time. That is the one Joan really wants. Joan turns off the ceiling fan. It was on low. Ceiling fans cool in summer and warm in winter. Joan and Walter have not sat outside on the patio for a long time. They have a screened-in patio so they would not even have to worry about the West Nile Virus. The placemats on the kitchen table wipe clean with a damp cloth. Joan goes back in the dining room. She sets the chair on all four legs. It did not scratch the buffet. Joan picks up her napkin. She sits down. Walter tells Joan that Rex was on the phone. Walter says he can go in an hour later if he wants. Walter finishes what he has on his plate. Joan says nobody touched the green bean supreme. Walter asks Joan what she bought for dessert. Joan says she got a Caramel Choc Bavarian. It has mousse-like creamy qualities on top of a biscuit crumb base. Walter says he has time for dessert if he goes in an hour later. Joan says the Caramel Choc Bavarian only takes 5-10 minutes to thaw. After it thaws, she just has to cut it into the desired number of servings. Walter and Joan talk about whether they should clean up before or after they have dessert. Joan says that she has all evening to clean up. They decide to clean up first. Walter and Joan's bisque dishwasher has space for fourteen place settings. Its sound package cleans the dishes without disrupting Walter and Joan's home. Joan asks Walter if he could bring in some wood. Joan says she would like to make a fire. Walter goes into the garage and puts on his work gloves. They feature anatomic relief pads to reduce calluses and loss of hand power. Walter carries in some wood and stacks it on the log rack. He makes three trips. The Caramel Choc Bavarian thaws out. Walter and Joan each have a piece of the Caramel Choc Bavarian. They eat at the kitchen table. It is round. Horns overflowing with corn, flowers, and fruit are depicted on the paper napkins. Walter wipes his mouth with the napkin. He goes to work. He bags groceries. He goes out and gets the carts from the parking lot. He looks up at the Jiffy Lube sign in the distance. It is all lit up. For a moment he forgets where he is. Walter just stands there in the middle of the parking lot. Joan walks upstairs. There are family pictures along the wall. Joan places her fingertips on one of the pictures. Brad is walking across a jungle gym beam in the picture. He is balancing on the jungle gym beam. His Speed Racer shirt was his favorite shirt. Joan goes all the way upstairs. Joan does things upstairs no one will ever know about. She shuts the door behind her. Joan locks herself in the master bath. Walter comes home from work earlier than expected. He will not be going back. The fire has gone out. The living room is dark. Walter sits down in the living room. Joan gets up early the next morning. The Meghans are already there when Joan arrives. They are sitting on the floor drinking huge sodas. They are wearing their high school sweatshirts. One customer alone buys over 25 jars. Claire calls on Saturday. Walter crams the rest of Brad's beer cans in 30-gallon stretchable strength trash bags. Joan puts the Christmas dinnerware back in the big and heavy china cabinet after the holidays. Walter reads a big, illustrated book about ants. Brad aces his first two tests. Walter grows a beard and takes a photography course at the community college. Joan applies for a loan. Claire gets tenure. Walter shaves and goes to the unemployment office. Claire cannot make it this summer. Joan's store goes in right next to a Deck the Walls. Brad learns about kinesiology. Walter's job is to inspect cleaning and sanitizing units at supermarkets and fast food establishments. He is a field service technician. Joan's sales are good. One Meghan helps out over Christmas break. When necessary Walter has to change the small measuring tips which regulate the flow of sanitizing fluid for the washing units, sanitizers, and cleaning dispensers. He carries fifteen color-coded measuring tips with him on his rounds. Honey Bee Good begins offering small gift items. Brad explores the power of proper breathing. Claire almost flies in for Easter. Brad takes an incomplete in Civil Procedure II. Walter fills out the inspection reports when he gets home. One bedroom is now his office. Meghan does not go back to college. Joan offers her a full-time job. Walter occasionally has to work out of town. He leaves Joan a note. Walter gets paid meals and hotels in addition to mileage. One of the two major retailers at the mall pulls out. Claire spends four days at home. Walter, Joan, and Claire go to Applebee's. They share starters. Meghan has a baby and reduces her hours. Walter observes how chicken gets breaded and fried. Joan pastes up large yellow signs on her storefront windows. *Everything Must Go!* Joan sometimes baby-sits Meghan's two children. Joan is present upon Brad's release. She holds him for a very long time. Joan says it is the happiest day of her life. Walter's car gets stolen on his inspection route in the city. The drunk black people say they did not see anything. Claire publishes her second book. Brad tries sales in a men's department. Joan joins the Red Hats Society. Walter quits his job. Brad's tribal totem tattoo by J-Man is his first. Joan expands her rooster and hen collection. Brad works at a gym for a short time. He gets better at body painting. Claire flies in every couple of years. Joan gets one last surprise visit from Meghan. The children bring her a candle made out of genuine bee's wax. It is naturally smokeless and dripless. Walter buys a new set of PINGs. He joins a senior's league. Brad gets a job as a prep cook. He places sacks and cases of up to 70 pounds in walk-in freezers. He works in a hot and damp environment. Joan drives the thirty miles to eat there once a week. She tells Brad that if there is anything he ever needs. Claire calls to say she got married. Joan has hip replacement surgery. Brad is not there one week. The manager has no idea. He says Brad just stopped showing up. Walter and Joan live until they are very old. Walter and Joan are living now. Walter is standing at the front door in his slippers. He is wearing a sweatshirt from where Claire teaches. He is paying the young, sweaty man from the lawn service. Joan is at the computer ordering groceries.

A Colt

It is gross. It is all wrinkly and used. Jimbone did not want to touch it at first. The lady in the picture has her eyes closed. She has blue eye shadow on. That is the only thing she has on. The gentleman behind her is ramming her from behind. He looks pretty intent and pleased. Jimbone is in his dad's Dodge Ram. It is in park. He is not about to go flying off the road from not watching the road and holes instead. The 2500 is the only heavy-duty pickup equipped with supplemental side-curtain air bags. Jimbone does not have his seatbelt properly fastened. When you go Ram, you grab life by the horns. The gentleman has the lady grabbed or held simultaneously by her shoulder and her tush. One of his hands is blurry. The photographer was not doing his job right. Jimbone is really focusing his attention in the Walgreen's parking lot. If only he could focus his attention like this in class. It is unexpectedly cold this evening, even for the middle of November. Not that Jimbone has been diagnosed as yet. But Jimbone does show signs of inattention, the specialist explained. Jimbone's parents really listened to what the specialist had to say. His dad was still alive at this point in time. Some kids at school call Jimbone Spacer because he sometimes spaces, but most people call Jimbone Jimbone. Everybody likes Jimbone. He plays left guard. His chief responsibilities are to protect Phil the quarterback and to create holes for the running backs. Jimbone also performs speed blocking. Jimbone hates being an ineligible receiver. He would love to catch a pass one day and score a touchdown one night under the lights. Jimbone would basically love to be a left tackle. Left tackles have to protect the quarterback on pass plays because most quarterbacks are right-handed and so when they throw, they have their backs turned on defenders coming from the left. Left tackles get paid more than right tackles. Jimbone is beginning to get warm in the cab. It is a Quad Cab with rear doors that open 85°, separating the 2500 from the pack. Jimbone feels good sitting up in the 2500. Jimbone's dad chose brilliant black crystal pearl with chrome wheel skins over infernal red crystal pearl with machine forged aluminum wheels with argent center caps, which is what his mom wanted, which they fought over because he had said she could get what she wanted this time. His mom thinks he is over at Timbone's studying for their history test. She really appreciates Timbone taking Jimbone under his wing, not that he really has wings. Jimbone's mom cannot keep up with everything anymore with Jim not being around anymore. Jimbone's mom hardly recognizes herself anymore when she looks in the mirror sometimes, which she tries not to do anymore. It will be two years already. Her hair looks thinner and brittler. Sometimes at work she takes off her headset when some customer starts yelling about a billing problem. Then she closes her eyes and asks herself why. Then she sees and feels the pain Jimbone's dad went through and how he was a trooper about it. Then she knows she is just going to have to keep going, too, because that is what Jim would want, and puts back on her headset and asks how she may help the customer according to the script she is to follow. He had been such an asshole to her for so long, but then when he was dying he suddenly became a loving husband and an inspiration to everyone. Everyone said how death really changed him. It brings tears to Jimbone's mom's eyes. It also put Jimbone's mom into a lot of debt. She does not know how she will ever pay it all off. She always thought the car dealership had this great coverage. She always thought Jim was the big sales stud there who carried the place, but they did not even close for the funeral. She still does not know the first thing about doing taxes. And now she also works mornings as a healthcare assistant. She recognized the nursing home smell right away and how the patients looked because it reminded her of Jim in the final stages of cancer of the tongue. She barfed the first day on the job and broke down. Jimbone can never keep all the dates straight and who fell off the boat and how many days they were on it and how Myles or Miles Standish was different from William Bradford and what was so special about Priscilla Mullins and what unrequited love is and how to spell all those Indian names except for Squanto and why you are not supposed to say squaw anymore, but Timbone can remember everything, and he also scammed a copy of last year's test. Timbone has been a Creamer for two months. He is the one who nominated Jimbone. You have to be nominated to become a Creamer. The four other Creamers are waiting at the other end of the parking lot in Tyler's mom's minivan. Tyler's mom's minivan is the perfect capacious vehicle to hang out in and pass around a bottle in. There are only four Creamers altogether. The Creamers is a selective club. Part of being a Creamer is sticking together and verifying the seed. It is the one thing that makes Creamers coalesce. The assistant principal is informed about the movement and is monitoring it closely. Everybody wants to be one now. Phil is in Tyler's minivan and says they should call Jimbone up. Phil is the one who still swears his class ring came off while fingering his girlfriend and that they had to wait until ragtime for it to come back out. Jimbone's cell starts ringing bars of I Like to Move It. It is from Madagascar, the movie. It surprises him. Jimbone was not expecting a call. His hand goes flying out of his pants. Tyler asks him what up and if he jizzed all over the steering wheel on accident or something. Jimbone says no. The steering column tilts. Then Tyler tells Jimbone to hurry up because he has to get the minivan home because his grandparents are in town and they are all going out to eat. Then Elliott grabs the phone and produces jerk-off noises with his cheek. Then they laugh and hang up, and Jimbone is once again all alone in the 2500. Jimbone's pecker is small again so he has to start all over again. Every page in the magazine is as good as the next. Jimbone lingers on one page that is crinklier than the others. Jimbone can see why. Then he senses it is time and gets out. He can see his breath. He points his key fob at the Ram and locks up. His shoes are supposed to be untied like that. This is a pretty big moment for Jimbone. He is keeping a firm grasp on his boner through his pocket so he does not lose it. Headlights flash and a car horn honks. Jimbone turns back in the direction of the headlights and the car honk. It is the guys. Jimbone sees raised fists sticking out of the windows. Jimbone pumps his fist back then turns back around. The doors to Walgreen's part and a gush of hot air hits him but does not mess up his hair because he has a hat on. It is up to Jimbone where he spills. It just has to be on the premises. It can end up on the floor, no problem. The deodorant aisle would be an ideal aisle, except for it is in the first aisle right by the doors. Because then Jimbone could look intent and confused on deciding between Arctic Force and Icy Blast, or between Surge and Fusion. That would give him plenty of time to blow. Jimbone is wearing his new letterman jacket. It demonstrates his school and team pride and his new varsity status. He is green and yellow all the way. He keeps it on in class all day except for in Mrs. Birch's class who has something up her A and does not allow jackets or hats in class even when you say you are cold or embarrassed about your new haircut. Jimbone decides the aisle he wants. He walks with determination right by the home repair aisle where it would probably just ooze down between the fine assortment of tools, and they would not be able to find it. Jimbone passes up the big bin with big bags of candy corn for 50% off. By the time he reaches the greeting card section his stiffy is history. That reminds him of his test tomorrow. Jimbone needs to get back on the ball. He looks left and right and steps up to the cards. It is like stepping up to a urinal. Jimbone is purposely not in front of the humor section, which would not be conducive. Those cards can get pretty funny and loud. You can open some of them and they make noises or play music. Jimbone has gone for the Inspirational-Grandparents-Pets section. Jimbone closes his eyes tight and grabs his weenie tight and tries to mentalize about *Holes*. He needs something in HD quality, and he needs it fast. That one crotch shot is starting to materialize that looked like it was taken down around her feet. Her toenails were polished. But the rest of her starts eluding Jimbone the more he moves up her parted and meaty legs. Jimbone is getting mental block just like he does in class all the time. He keeps envisioning the antique car show they always went to when he was a kid. Jimbone opens his eyes. The character Maxine is playing a banjo on the card right in front of him. She says to party your butt off. Next to Maxine is a card with a picture of a feather falling onto a pool of water. One card has dog doo on it, and one card is the one his dad gave him right before he died. That freaks Jimbone out. It is still in circulation. It was in an envelope, and Jimbone was not supposed to open it until after. It had a letter in it. Jimbone almost has it memorized because of all the times he read it. The boy on the card is flying a kite. It is sunny out. The card tells you to keep your spirit and heart forever young. His dad's printing looked real shaky because he was real sick. Dear Champ. I'm real sorry I have to be writing and giving you this card. I feel like I'm really letting you down. Because I always thought I would be there for you to help you out and watch you grow up and make your dreams come true. But I guess that was not in the cards, huh? But I want you to know how proud I am of you and how much I love you. You're the greatest! And have meant everything to me in my life. Like remember the time you knocked that homer over the fence and instead of rounding the bases you ran up to me in the bleachers? That's one memory I'm definitely taking with me. You can bet on that. And I'm going to be watching out for you, so you better watch out. Okay? And do me a favor and look after Mom. Alright? Don't give her too much trouble, more than she already has. Thanks. Otherwise just always do your best. That's all you can do is go in there swinging. And remember that I'll always love you. Go for it, Jimbone! Love, Dad. Jimbone has the card up on his bulletin board thing. He has it right in the middle, right between his football team picture and one of Peyton Manning passing.

Pie

Scot's Earglove Flex fits comfortably over both ears. When his one ear gets tired or hot or itchy or just plain tired, Scot just puts it on his other ear. You slip the Flex on and off. You do not clip it on and off. That is the Flex's big comfort advantage. Scot's ears do not look red or chaffed at all. You cannot tell how long Scot has been in meetings today. With Earglove Flex you can have intense meetings anywhere you want to and anytime. Scot is having an intense meeting right on his bed. His old Milwaukee Brewers trashcan is right there next to his bed. His old Milwaukee Brewers bedspread is right there on his bed. The Home Builders and Garden Show is starting tomorrow. That is what all these intense meetings are all about. Scot runs his hand through his hair with its volumizing foam styler that makes his hair look naturally wavy. You benefit from its combination of superior botanical ingredients. Scot's semi-casual clothes always look nice and baggy. It has been a real long week. The weekend is going to be real longer. His six Milwaukee Brewers wool pennants are arranged on the wall facing his bed to look like a pie. Each pennant is a piece of the pie. Each pennant is stitched with the Milwaukee Brewers iconic glove and ball. Jorge tells Scot that almost every convention has at least one booth discrepancy and to start getting used to it. Jorge says booth discrepancy is just part of the fucking job. Smith's Power Shower & Sunsetter Awnings and All Tucked In have both been erroneously allotted Booth #529. Foot traffic is heavy around Booth

#529. It is near enough to the restrooms to get the extra foot traffic, but far enough away not to get the odors. All Tucked In is a bedding and linens store your spouse may be familiar with. Scot keeps wondering about conventions. It seems to Scot that with conventions it seems like it is just one convention after another. Conventions never stop. Conventions only want to fool people into buying their shit. Jorge tells Scot to get hold of Smith and to get hold of him now and to fix the fucking problem and not to get back to him until he does, but then to get back to him immediately. That is how the meeting ends. Scot can finally get off his Flex for a second and rub his ear, not that it is red or chafed or anything. Scot keeps wondering lately about more than just conventions. For Scot it is like everything all of a sudden. It is the system. The system is the real problem. The system never cares about the environment even when it says it does. The system never cares about human dignity even when it says it does. And Jorge the beaner is no different. Scot gets up off his bed. He sizzles this Nerf against the wall. It is so light and made-for-indoors that nothing happens. It does not make any of his rocks or gems fall out of his rock and gem display case. Scot walks to his door that is closed and bends down and looks at himself in the mirror stuck to the door. Then he opens the door and walks to the bathroom. Scot is in his thick, white socks. Scot can tell no one is home and goes to the bathroom. He sits down so as to avoid splash. Scot stands up and flushes, then flushes his face in cold water and looks at his face in the mirror and sees how wet it is. Scot dries his face in a thick and plush towel that smells good and fresh. He goes downstairs and through the hearth room and through the island kitchen. He sits down in the breakfast room on a chair. Scot is so sick of Booth #529. Five-two-nine is all he has heard all day. Five-two-nine is all he has said all day. The sun is not shining into the breakfast room because it faces east to capture the morning sun. It is currently a little after 4 p.m. Scot stares blankly out the window at the air-conditioning system that is right outside the window. A brown bird has perched on it and is looking around. Maybe it is looking for a worm. Maybe it is looking for a colorful tail. Scot shakes the box of Yogos Rollers Cha-Cha Cherry. They are almost gone, but there are some left. That is the kind of shake sound it makes. The fruit-flavored breakfast snacks with chewy centers and creamy yoghurt coating are an excellent source of calcium. Scot sticks his hand and arm down in the box and digs around and grabs a few and eats a few. That one brown bird flies off to some place else. Maybe it has found what it is looking for. Maybe someone tried to shoot it. Maybe the AC kicked on. The new AC unit is up to 40% quieter than the old AC unit. Now you do not even know when the AC is on or not. Scot suddenly realizes he hates Cha-Cha Cherry, but he does not make a mess about it or dropkick the box or anything. Scot goes to where the medicine is and swallows two Tylenol and puts the bottle back. Then he takes the bottle back out and swallows one more and puts it back. Scot wants temporary relief from his aches and pains. There, he feels a little better. He looks around where he is in the hearth room. He sticks his hand up in the ceiling fan on low. Scot goes downstairs to the rec room in the basement. Scot needs some kind of something, some kind of outlet maybe. Scot looks all around the rec room and sits down at Ab Lounge 2. This could be the right kind of something, the right kind of outlet. Then Scot will move on to Smith and take care of Smith. He will tell Smith it is either Booth #488 or adios amigo. Then he will move on to Jorge. Scot pushes real hard and his face turns red. But Ab Lounge 2 ends up not being the right kind of something. It is the wrong outlet. Something is wrong with Scot's obliques. They are probably just too flaccid is the problem. Scot is not going to start playing air hockey alone. The rec room is getting too cold anyway. Scot goes back upstairs to his room, but then goes back to his bathroom. He strips down and stands sideways in front of the bathroom mirror and pulls in his gut and makes some derogatory remark about his boob things. Today is Friday. It is supposed to be T.G.I.F. It is not supposed to be this. It is not supposed to be five-two-nine five-two-nine five-to-nine. Scot wants to know why college only lasts like 10 or 11 semesters. Scot takes another shower. His shower caddy has an array of body washes. His body washes range from extra fresh and deep clean to clean comfort. But this afternoon all talk of clean and fresh makes him sick. Scot just stands there under the water until his skin turns light pink. Then Scot gets out and rubs down. Scot gets the water out of his ears and puts back on his same clothes because they were not dirty to begin with. He stares at himself straight in the mirror and gives himself this big, fake, phony smile. Conventions are already getting to him. They are making him big and fake and phony. Scot turns off the light and the heat lamp and goes back to his room. His cell phone is right where he left it. It is right on his clipboard. His clipboard is right where he left it. His laptop is right where he left it. Scot picks up his cell phone and wakes it up. There are three new messages from Jorge. He knew there would be. He thought there would be five. He thought there would be two thousand. Scot has this neat Brewers T.V. pillow on his bed. Scot sits down on his bed and props himself up against his Brewers T.V. pillow and sort of half-lays, half-sits there. He stares at his cell phone and starts counting down from ten. Jorge calls him by the time he gets to the number 6. Scot answers. Jorge wants to know where the fuck he has been and why he has not returned his fucking calls and what the fuck is up with Smith. Scot goes that Smith is cool with four-eight-eight and that he was just down faxing him the new terms and that that is where he was and that that is why he has not returned his calls. Jorge says cool especially since four-eight-eight sucks and how that no one ever wants four-eight-eight and says that he just needs that confirm fax once Scot gets it from Smith. Scot says no prob. Scot says Smith said he was going to confirm and fax immediately. Jorge says how there has now been a rescheduling for tomorrow morning. Jorge says the Humane Society seminar focusing on safety for your pet and family had to be bumped up and that Scot is going to have to moderate it. He says that Scot needs to be in by 8 and then will also moderate the dog adoption right after that. Jorge says how that otherwise Sparky the Clown and Friends would not have enough time to entertain kids and parents alike with ballooning, face painting, and games. Scot goes sure. He says he likes dogs. Scot is conducting a search. Jorge says that Scot does not have to like dogs. He says that he just has to moderate the adoption. Scot goes sure. Jorge says how he will be tied up Saturday morning. Jorge has to personally pick up Matt Fox and Shari Hiller at the airport. They are arguably the most recognized home-decorating personalities in America. Their home-decorating program is a real show about real decorating for real people. Jorge wants to know if Scot is even listening to a fucking word he is saying. Scot says how his parents watch Matt and Shari all the time. Jorge says to just fax him that Smith confirm and to be in no later than 7:45. Scot has searched Valerie before. He has searched her like 20 times. She is still not on Facebook for some weird reason. Scot could still find her number though. Scot used to call her sometimes back in college. In Valerie's new time zone it is not even late. It is not a Friday night phone call or anything. It is not even Friday evening where she is. It is like Friday afternoon. Scot readjusts his Brewers T.V. pillow until it feels better and right. He slips his Flex back on. Scot taps his clipboard with the back end of the pen so the tip goes in and out. Scot stares at the pie on the wall. And then Valerie is suddenly there. She is right there in his ear. She is right there in his room. She says hello. Then it sounds like the phone falls to the floor. It bangs around real loud in Scot's ear. Scot catches a sort of whine or blabber in the background. Then Valerie is back again right in his ear. Her voice is the same. He cannot describe it or anything. It just is. It is just hers. Valerie says hello and sorry. Then Valerie says hello again and asks if anybody is there. Scot says hi and if that is Valerie. Valerie says yes. You can tell from her voice she is wondering who wants to know. Even Scot wonders who wants to know. Who is this Scot who wants to know? Scot says hi again and hey and that it is him Scot Belcher if she remembers. Scot says that one Scot from that one Western Civ class back in college. Scot says they studied together sometimes at the library. Scot says he was the one Scot that spelled his name with one T. Scot says. Valerie is like oh. She is like yeah. She is like Scot Belcher how weird college. Scot says he knows how it is probably pretty weird. He says that how that that was why he almost did not. Valerie asks Scot to hold on a sec. She seems to talk to somebody else that seems to be in the room. Scot thinks he hears her saying upsy or maybe whoopsie. Then Valerie is back again. She says sorry again and asks Scot if he is out on the west coast, too, or something and how he got her number. Scot says no actually and that he is still back you know in. Valerie asks Scot to hold on just one more sec. Scot says or is about to say, but he hears the phone being put down on a hard surface. It could be the kitchen counter. It could be the chopping block. Valerie is back again for like already the third time in like one minute. Valerie says she has a little squirmy wormy Madison who does not like Mommy to talk on the phone does she. Scot says oh and how that if it is a bad time that. Valerie says it is fine as long as he does not mind and if he is with the alumni association or something. Scot says great and okay and no actually about the alumni association but how actually he just moved because he got this new job? Valerie congratulates him. Scot says no and how it is not really you know that great and how he basically just works the phone and. Madison must be hungry and needs her jar of peaches. Valerie gets her her jar of peaches and her special spoon. Her special spoon is bent in such a way that it cannot be swallowed. Both Valerie and her husband have tried to swallow the spoon and were unable to. Scot says and anyway. He says that on account of the new job and when he moved and had to move back. He says well wherever and that he came across all this old college stuff and that one Western Civ reader if she remembers that one. Valerie says she does. She says she does a little bit. She says that it is just that at the moment with Madison and everything. Scot says right and gotcha. Scot asks Valerie if she remembers that one time they were studying at the library café and where those two black janitor guys got in that knife fight. Valerie says oh and that is right and how awful that was the blood. Scot says it was a gore-fest and all those tables and lattes tipping over. Valerie says you were a hungry little bird weren't you. Scot says huh and then oh yeah and then that that day that happened with the knife fight they were trying to write that Karl Marx paper if she remembers. Valerie says not really and that basically she just remembers his beard and that she kind of has to get going here soon. Scot says he understands and that he is at work, too. He says but anyway he started reading that big fat reader again in his spare time lately. He says he even went to the public library and checked out a Karl Marx biography. Scot says his public library in town has a café too now. Scot says but anyway. Valerie says but anyway what? Scot says that with all the reading he has been doing. He says he kind of started thinking about that class again and kind of was thinking about her again sort of. Scot waits for some kind of reaction. Madison burps or spits up. Valerie says oh you little piggy and that she sees. She says she thinks she should probably go now. Scot employs Valerie's name and says just a sec. He says the point. He says the point is that he was reading Marx this very morning and came across that one quote. Valerie says she is sorry but. She says if he is not from the alumni. Scot says it was the same quote that they were reading that day and trying to understand and trying to write that one group one-page paper about and that it was just him and her in the group and that that was what they were working on that afternoon in the library café when those two black guys started knifing each other. Valerie says Scot listen she does not apprec. Scot says and that reading that quote really made him think, and think of her and what she was wearing that day and that he just wants to read her the quote. Valerie says she really does not. Valerie asks Scot how he got her number. Scot says the internet. Valerie says but how her name has changed. She says she thinks her husband is done cutting the lawn and is. Scot asks to just let him read her the quote. Once Madison burped or spit up she fell right to sleep. Madison is sleeping soundly on Valerie's shoulder. Scot says the production of too many useful things results in too many useless people. Scot asks Valerie if she remembers that quote and that assignment. He says he happens to have their paper right here in front of him on his clipboard and that he could even read it to her. He says it is only one page. Valerie says no not really and that she really. Scot says okay and that he understands. Valerie says thanks and that it was nice that he you know but that you know. Then Scot says that he just regrets that he never asked her out when he had the chance and now he is in conventions. Then Scot blurts out that he only realizes now how much he was in love with her and how he blew his chance with her and that he could even fly out there and they could maybe. The line gets all muffled. It is like under water or under a big thick sweatshirt or under a sweaty palm. Then there is this male voice on the line. It wants to know who is calling and what the hell they want. Scot hangs up. To hang up all you need to do is press the red button. Scot leaves his Flex on because he is so out of it and dazed and does not realize he has it on. He hears some noise and looks out his window. The girl across the street is practicing her free throws. She shoots a hundred every day around this time of day. Scot's parents say she is only a sophomore but is already on the varsity squad. She is almost six feet tall. Scot's cell rings. He sees it is Jorge and presses the red button. Scot has watched her sink over 80 out of a hundred and how they kept going right through the hoop without ever even touching the hoop. Scot thinks how, how small hoops are. Scot's cell rings again. He says yo Jorge s'up. Jorge says where the fuck is the fax and that he needs that fax before he can leave the office tonight and that he wants to leave. Scot says dude he sent it and that he should already have it. Jorge says he does not have it. Jorge says Scot probably sent it to the wrong fucking number again and to resend it to his number. Scot gazes at the woolly pie. Jorge says Scot and if he is even there. Scot says how did you get my number. Jorge is like what the and who the fuck he is even talking about. Scot says. There is a knock on Scot's door. Scot tells Jorge to hold on a sec. He pushes the red button to make Jorge history. Scot goes to come on in. Scot's mom comes on in. She is wearing a foliage-print blouse and a scarf-like accessory around her neck. She says she hopes she is not interrupting. Scot goes heck no and how that he was just finishing up and how that it is TGIF. Scot's mom says great and how that that is her Scot and that Dad is home from the offices and that dinner is almost ready. Scot goes yum dinner. Scot's mom says great and how that that is her Scot and that she tried out a new recipe. She says she made grilled tangy sole.

The Body Manager

The Body Manager is cleverly multi-functional. It is red and clipped to his pants. Roger prefers a classic fit which eases through the seat and thigh. Roger used to prefer a relaxed fit which added room in the seat and thigh. Roger has changed since being let go. He has lost weight. He believes he is shorter than he has been in years. The Body Manager has several ergonomic buttons. Its current reading is 844. The average body requires 9000 steps per day for a healthy mind and body. Roger has a long way to go according to the Body Manager. It cost four box tops plus $5. Today is hump day, and Roger has a long, steep hump ahead of him. Visibility is low. It is fall. Once again Roger is standing at the living room window. The paper is lying on the front lawn which has a gentle slope to it. And to think that they were discussing relandscaping not too long ago. Wendy wanted a pergola more than anything. She wanted theirs to be ample enough to have plants or accessories on all sides and still have enough room to walk through and enjoy. It was only going to take 20 minutes to assemble. The journal is in a plastic yellow sleeve. It is full of news, events, and sports from around the world and close to home. So many things are happening without Roger all around him. It makes Roger want to explode. The For Sale sign panel is printed on both sides. Roger can read it from inside the house. It serves as a constant reminder of economic meltdown and bad luck. Janey is bringing a potential buyer over this afternoon. She has real good vibes about the couple. Janey says to keep trusting her vibes even though her vibes about the last couple were way off. It was a lesbian couple. Janey always carries that real huge three-ring binder around with her. The grass could almost use another mowing. Roger's turf will not stop growing. It is almost unreal. Across the street Ray is climbing up into his beast. He is in pharmacy packaging and supplies. He says he always hated chemistry class. He says he never understood or memorized the periodic table. He says he never even took chemistry in college. But then he says to look at him now. Ray is one big asshole more on the sales and distribution side of things. He is a frequent flyer. He backs out of the driveway and honks his musical horn. Today he honks Row, Row, Row Your Boat. The Body Manager challenges you to walk around the room when you talk on the phone. Roger knows how to fool the Body Manager which dares you to do another lap around the mall. Roger's phantom pains have been coming and going without warning ever since his former employer took huge losses and had to act accordingly. He has a can of Pledge in his hand. Shiny wood surfaces help his home come alive. His dust cloth's grab and hold technology uses electrostatic charges to lock onto dust, dirt, and hair. Roger's dust cloth does not merely move dust around. It removes it. Roger takes satisfaction in knowing he is not just pushing dust off the edges of furniture and into the air. He wants dust gone. Roger wipes the square accent table with chunky legs. The main thing is to keep busy, to not let yourself go, and to keep yourself together. Another main thing is to not dwell on the happiness and upward mobility of others, your wife, for example. There is a ceramic inn resting on the middle of it. A small couple is standing outside the inn, their glasses raised. They look happy. The wine looks real. You can almost hear them saying toast. Roger can. Roger says toast. Even when doing things like cleaning the house and doing the laundry, Roger can get pretty bitter. He can ask himself some of the hard questions. Roger unplugs the inn. It has a light that lights the lights up when you switch on the switch. The inn suddenly goes dark, but the couple does not seem to notice. They are having way too much fun. They are oblivious to suffering. Maybe they are just plain drunk. Drunk on wine and drunk on life itself. Roger picks up the inn and carries it through the living room. It is light-weight and has those fuzzy things underneath to protect vulnerable surfaces from scratching. He steps on a rattle on his way into the kitchen. Bills and flatware are lying on the island. The traffic helicopter is on on the radio. Roger walks up to the trashcan. It is touchless. Sometimes it opens and closes when no one is even near. Or else every single time you walk by it. It can be a great conversation piece if the people living with it still talk to each other. It is stainless steel. It keeps your hands clean. It requires four D batteries. Roger releases the inn and watches it tumble into the trashcan. Since it is a cozy little inn, it easily fits in the trashcan. Roger watches the lid close after precisely three seconds. He tries to resume dusting. But Roger is just not into it. He hears the retarded bus drive by. It appears as though he is trying to tear the dust cloth to pieces. But the dust cloth is tear-free. Something in Roger seems to be either snapping or cracking. It has nothing to do with that ceramic inn per se. Roger actually likes wine. He appreciates it. It just happened to be at the wrong place at the wrong time. Roger crunched numbers for over twelve fucking years. Try to imagine what that is like. He rests his hand on the newel post. Maybe he is going to shake it down and rip it right off. He does not do it. Roger walks upstairs and consults the Body Manager at the top of the stairs. It does not give you more points or steps for inclines. Roger looks into little Todd's room. Todd is slumbering away. His mouth is open. Todd looks just like Wendy. That is what everybody says. Nobody ever says Todd resembles Roger. Todd's head is resting on a Go Diego Go sham. Todd appears to like Diego who is swinging from a vine. Roger picks up the pacifier that closes automatically when dropped so the nipple always stays clean and also promotes healthy oral development.

He puts it in his pocket. He fixes Todd's cover. He walks back downstairs. He puts on a windbreaker. It does not have his name on the back. Roger locks the front door behind him. Roger and Wendy have their autumn porch décor up. Decks are the big thing now, but you still need porch décor. Their porch décor has nothing that adolescents might feel compelled to steal or smash and destroy. Janey thinks it looks welcoming and great. Roger walks down the street on the sidewalk. He watches out for sprinklers on automatic timer. Roger knows who has an in-ground irrigation system and who does not. Roger looks just like one of the neighborhood walkers out for a casual walk, not a Nordic walk. Roger turns left and sees a row of cars parked along the curb. He cannot get over why Wednesdays are such big garage sale days. This garage sale comes all the way out down the driveway. Snow tires are stacked up at the end of the driveway. The largest items are in the front yard. There are mainly old people there and mothers with small children. Roger purchased snow tires last fall and then it hardly even snowed. They are only asking four dollars for the weed whacker, but that is because it is one that requires bumping. Little baby food jars full of anchors, screws, nails, and nuts are arranged on a small card table. Todd's favorite baby food is baby peaches. They make his poop smell extra bad. He could eat them breakfast, lunch, and dinner. There is a clothes rack where each item is one dollar and some cardboard boxes with books. Roger has never minded reading a good book. What Roger does not like is boring books and space adventures. Roger is almost starting to feel warm in his windbreaker. He gets asked if he would like some coffee. The guy is offering him a cup, one of those white Styrofoam cups that almost never decompose. Roger tells him he has the day off. The guy says he loves hosting garage sales. He says that it gets him out of the house, that he is a consultant, that he works from home, that he writes off his entire office, and that he has a couple of red-eared sliders up in his office. He says the way they bask for hours under the heat lamps is meditative for him. He says the way they never move helps him work. He goes to help another customer. Roger remains up by the coffee maker and where you pay. It is in a classic metal lunch box. Roger tries to open it up with one hand but is unable to get it open. He looks around and over at the crock pot. There are games on a coffee table. Yahtzee and Connect Four are there, and something called Amun-Re and Advanced Squad Leader are there. Uno is there. Roger hears somebody ask if the hangers are included in the price. Two kids are jumping up and down on the bed in the front lawn. Then Roger is back up by the classic metal lunch box. The guy says that he sees he has found something. He tells Roger it still even has the original directions, but that two destroyers are missing. He says it is vintage, minus the destroyers. He says him and his bro used to play all the time. He says they played so much all the time that they were practically calling out coordinates like B8 in their sleep. Roger pays and leaves. He takes the game with. He takes the shortcut that goes between two houses and that leads straight into the park. Roger is in the park. The park is a large parkland with a family aquatic pool complex, athletic fields, horseshoe courts, concession stands and more. It is not the first thing he does, but one of the first things he does is he throws away the Body Manager. He throws it away without any triumphant gesture. He does not raise his fist in the air or scream and say yeah. He does not give his wife the finger for basically telling him to wear it. Roger just unclips it and drops it into the big metal receptacle. He helps keep America clean. He goes and sits down by the tennis courts. Lights still only cost a quarter if you want to play at night and get eaten alive. Few people do anymore. Roger has a wimpy second serve like most guys. To think that Roger made the high school all-star team right here on this court and then to look at him now. Roger becomes introspective with Battleship in his lap. The sun inches across the sky up above the clouds which are back. A policeman asks Roger what he is doing. It startles Roger. It makes him jump.

Roger did not see or hear the policeman coming. He wants to know what Roger is doing sitting alone on a bench in the middle of the park. Roger says he is out for a walk. He shows the policeman what he just purchased at a garage sale. The policeman wants some I.D. He scrutinizes Roger's I.D. once he gives it to him. The policeman tells him to get on his way. Then the policeman gets a call in and leaves. Roger grips his head in his hands like he is going to pull it off with his hands. He is unsure whether he should take his board game with. First he does not. Then he turns back and does. The hill is real steep. Roger is fortunate to be going down it. An arrow is spray-painted on it to tell cross-county runners which way to go. It is a brutal sport. Cheerleaders could care less about you. They never decorate your locker before a race. Roger crosses the street and hopes nobody whizzes anything at him from their car. They call it pegging. Roger feels something is wrong and keeps walking. Lowe's is doing great business. You would never guess a trailer park used to be here and got bought out. Somebody named Craig is being called to lumber over the intercom. Roger nears the overpass. He has never walked over an overpass before. A sign up ahead says it is time for a chalupa. Another sign up ahead says Jewelry. There is a steady flow of traffic. The Greyhound station is at the Conoco station. Roger sees all the black people lined up in a line. Roger gets in the back of the line. There is no way he is going to butt here. Once you buy your ticket, you wait outside by the air machine and wait for the bus to come. Everybody seems to know everybody. A lot of people are carrying cardboard boxes instead of luggage. Roger sees several pillows. The junk food they are eating looks good. A little old man in a fedora starts talking to Roger. He keeps saying he is boogalooing and blaséing. They are hard words to spell. Roger does not know what on earth he is talking about. Roger buys a ticket from the lady at the window. She looks it up where he says he wants to go to. She says she does not book too many tickets for up north. She says he will have to transfer in Hays. She says he will have to wait about six hours in Hays. She says Hays is not as bad as people say Hays is. She says to go and eat at Muddy's and to try their black crappie. She says the trip will take thirty-one hours all told. She asks if he has any bags. Roger shows her his Battleship. She says they can go ahead and tag it, but that he can go ahead and keep it with him if he wants. Roger enters the minimart. He has not had a Little Debbie in years. He wishes he was nine again and a kid again and back in third grade and life could start all over again. This time around he would go into marketing. The bus pulls in. It makes a hissing sound as it comes to a complete stop. Some people de-board. They will be allowed to re-board first and are entitled to keep their seat. They look tired, lonely, and poor, just like Roger thought they would. He once learned that he is one of the 35 million descendents of the Mayflower passengers. Everybody puts their baggage by the huge baggage compartment door that opens upwards, not out. There is no pushing or shoving during the boarding process. Roger gets a window seat. They are tinted panorama windows. He reclines and looks out across the street at a low, pale brick building. The letters for Furniture World are up where the letters for Tires and Breaks used to be. At first Roger cannot get the stupid footrest to work. Then he does and relaxes. The bus breaks down after like only three miles. Roger must have dozed off. Some of the passengers just laugh about it. You are supposed to stay seated, but some passengers get out to see what is wrong. Roger can see the mall where him and Wendy used to go shopping at. A lot of times he would just wait for her in the food court. He is one of the last people on the bus. Then he de-boards, too. Everybody is keeping well to the shoulder. Everybody is talking about what the problem could be. Smoke is not pouring from the engine. The passengers stand around and call their relatives or friends or the prison to say they are going to miss their appointed time slot and ask what they can do about it. Roger walks away. He figures forget it. He can hear people calling after him to stop and to come back. Roger gets off the highway at the first exit. He walks up the off ramp and past the yield sign and sees another sign for chalupas. Roger is really going to have to try one. At the first light Roger makes a right into Blockbuster. The mounted TVs are all showing the same blockbuster. Roger asks the man behind the counter for an application because he says he saw the sign in the window. He points with his thumb back over his shoulder to where he thinks the sign is. The man behind the counter is the manager who asks him if he could start today at 4:00. Roger looks at his watch and says yes. Brian says awesome. Roger tells him his name. Brian sizes Roger up and says he might even take a small and goes to get him a shirt and comes back and says that all they have are larges. He says Roger will just have to tuck it in until he orders some more and they arrive. Brian says they can worry about the paperwork when he comes back at 4:00. Brian tells Roger to make sure to wear tan pants and dark shoes. Then Brian just wants to make sure that Roger does like movies. Roger says he does, and Brian says awesome. Brian tells Roger he thinks he will like it here and that they get free popcorn. Then Roger goes and does the same thing at Best Buy and Office Depot. Each place gives him a shirt to wear. Roger really hit the right exit. No place gives him pants. Roger starts later today at each place. He does not press his luck at Pier 1. Wendy got some home accents from there. The decorative willow spheres on their tabletops are from there. Roger runs across the road without getting hit and enters the Red Roof Inn. The young, attractive receptionist with long, straight blond hair greets him from behind the counter. She has large silver hoop earrings. Roger sees all the room keys hanging behind her, except that they are not keys. They are like flat plastic credit cards. Roger wants to inquire about their Red Hot Deals. He is on the verge of asking for a single room. He envisions himself living on Westfield Mall Drive right across from the mall. He could walk the mall every morning. He could meet someone new. The receptionist says sir? She hates it when goons like this come in. Roger asks the receptionist if he may use the phone. Roger says his car broke down out there and that something happened to it and that he needs to use the phone and how that he forgot to recharge his cell phone this morning. Roger has AAA Premier, which includes one free tow of up to 200 miles. The receptionist calls his attention to the pay phone located just outside the doors. Roger calls a taxi. It takes forty minutes to get there. It is a humongous old blue boat. The back seat is saggy and scummy and also a little bouncy and rocky. Roger stares out the window on his familiar way home. The radio announcer comes on and says that that last one was from Ricky Skaggs's classic Highways and Heartaches. Roger gives the driver everything in his wallet. Janey has left a card on the front door with the No Show box ticked. He unlocks the door. He thinks how glad he is that he did not throw his keys away when he almost did back at the park. They were gripped tight in his hand. He was about to rear back and throw them as far as he could out past the infield. Roger runs upstairs to check on Todd, his son. Todd is lying peacefully on his back. His eyes are wide open and inquisitive. He is staring up at the Rainforest Peek-a-boo Leaves Mobile. It brings the magic of the rainforest to Todd's crib. It provides music, motion, and lights like in a real rain forest. Roger picks Todd up out of his crib and holds him tightly because he loves him. His diapers need changing. Roger remembers the pacifier in his pocket and takes it out of his pocket and gives it to Todd. Roger gets a bottle going and looks what he can make for lunch. Then he has to change Todd again because after his bottle he always does. He puts on some Baby Mozart and sits next to Todd and taps his foot. But when Wendy goes and calls and says she will be working late again tonight

Fear's

Arms and Armor is located in halls 125-128. It is an exhibit. He thought Arms and Armor was going to kick. He is Wayne. Wayne walks back and forth through the halls all day long. His uniform is dark blue. He is unarmed, not allowed to sit down, steal, or trash any property. Sometimes he sits down. Arms and Armor is on the lower level. It is very quiet on the lower level. There is hardly ever a sound on the lower level. That is how boring it is. The lights in the halls are dimmed, but the display cases are real bright. Wayne can never stay awake. Visitors can reach the exhibit by taking the stairs or the elevator. The elevator makes an agreeable ring when the doors open. That is one sound. Another sound is the water fountain. Those are basically the two sounds all day long. Wayne already stood Ottoman Embroideries of the 18th and 19th Centuries. Floral motifs predominated: tulips, hyacinths, carnations, bouquets of roses, and cypress trees. They played an integral part in special occasions, like weddings and rites of passages. Wayne wanted to be a gaming surveillance officer more than anything in the whole world. It was his dream. He wanted to observe casino operations for irregular activities. He wanted to monitor casino floors from a catwalk located over one-way mirrors. Then Same-Day Detox Kit did not work. It did not come through for him. Wayne has a static security position and opportunities for advancement are limited. It is a beautiful, big museum up on a hill. You can go there for free if you want. The sallet helmet Wayne is standing next to dates from the late 15th century. The metalworker beat it from one large sheet of metal. He had only hammers, anvil irons, and raw muscle power at his disposal. It could deflect blows on the battle field. After two months all sallet helmets look pretty much the same. The adjoining hall is full of flintlocks and the Swiss crossbow and the musket from Germany. Wayne can sometimes get a good war going in his head if he daydreams hard enough where people get blown apart, mini-marts get pillaged, and one time a three-wheeler literally started to like melt. Wayne gets off in another 25 minutes. The last 25 minutes take forever. Then he is done. It is real bright outside. Art students are sitting drawing on the steps and are all fags. Wayne's front car door still needs feathering and priming. He gets stuck in traffic on his way home. Then he goes to where he goes every day after work, or almost every. It is where Drug Emporium used to be. People park their cars there now who are trying to sell them, and then other people come by and look at them and maybe buy one. It works for everyone. Wayne is next to the silver Omega going for $1200. Wayne feels it is overpriced. He feels the dick is never going to get it. Wayne sits there. He sees everything. He does not miss anything. He saw her walking back home from Wal-Mart one time. That was the best time. The little houses behind Wal-Mart look even littler next to Wal-Mart. She was less than 250 feet away. She had on jeans and those white heels and was carrying some bags and was pushing a stroller and kept having to kick one wheel that did not seem to be working properly. He wanted to help her but was not allowed to by law. Trashing her mailbox that one time really alienated her. Things were never the same after that. She just stood there watching him do it. Which really egged him on. It really pissed him off. Wayne can see her house from his spot. It has big, green, bushy shrubs on the side of the carport. They are big, green, and bushy and look hard to trim. Skipper is probably behind them in the back yard right now, chasing his tail and just being himself. He gave her that dog. Sometimes her husband comes out and smokes on the porch. In summer he wears shorts. In fall he wears pants. In winter he wears a winter jacket. Then when it is summer again he wears shorts again. He always has the same orange hat on no matter when. Then he goes back inside and has her body all to himself. John is sweeping the floor. John starts by the door and works his way back to the back. A bell over the door rings when the door opens. It rang three times today. He did a temple fade and a high and tight today for someone who wants to get back into the Marines, and the mailman came by. John and the mailman get along. He offered the mailman a free haircut. John likes to cut hair. He loves it. He does not know even why. That is why John guesses he is a barber. He looks out the door and sees his new barber pole. It is the slowly revolving symbol that is recognized by millions of people all over the world. John switches the sign on the door to *Closed* and pushes the broom around the three barber chairs with adjustable headrests. It is the end of John's day. If John could feasibly cut hair twenty-two or twenty-three hours a day, he might. There is a pair of thinning shears in his smock. It keeps the hair off. John interrupts his sweeping and looks up at the TV. But it is not a plasma TV. It is up in the corner so everybody can see it. Kolby Ungeheuer is tied for third with Hunter Herrin after the first round. Wade White is in the box. Wade is from Richfield, Wisconsin, a town located just minutes outside of the Milwaukee metropolitan area, and really wants his first IPRA world title. The calf bolts from the chute. It takes off. John watches it run like mad. Then Wade starts to pursue it with pigging string clenched in his teeth. Wade makes the catch and dismounts because he was on a horse. He sprints to the calf and flanks it. He ties three of the legs with the pigging string in good time. The calf does not kick free. It wants to, though. You can tell. Then it is Jerome Schneeberger's turn. Then it is Tate Watkins's turn. Then it is Garrett Nokes's turn. Then it is Blake Lauer's turn. The tie-down roping championship is scheduled to go on for hours. John could watch it for hours. He has a largemouth bass mounted on the wall. It is a right turn, tail down largemouth bass. John would ultimately like to have a whole mounted bass collection on his wall. On this wall. John thinks that would look neat in his barber shop, which just opened. It is called Fear's Barber Shop because John's last name is Fears. It is kind of a funny name for a barber shop because you are not supposed to be afraid. Many regard fish taxidermy as the most difficult branch of taxidermy. It is the one area of wildlife art where the artist must totally recreate the colors of the skin all over the animal. Like in bird taxidermy, the taxidermist only has to paint the legs, feet, and bill. And like in mammal taxidermy, the taxidermist only has to paint the nose and eyes. But like in fish taxidermy the taxidermist has to paint every square inch of the specimen. John wipes off the hot lather machine and refills his frosted spray bottle decorated with shear designs. John sits down, watches as the second round gets underway, and piddles with a neck duster. Joe Beaver is first. His career earnings top $2 million, and he also runs a rental property business. Wayne knocks on the door. John gets up and lets Wayne in, and he comes in. Wayne grabs a magazine off the magazine rack. It was hard for John to decide what kind of magazine rack to get because wall-mounted magazine racks save space, but John wanted to save his wall space. So he chose a free-standing display rack. He asks Wayne if he saw his new barber pole out there, and he says he did. John says he thinks it looks pretty cool. He looks at it some more. He says he still cannot believe he has his own barber pole. John walks back around to his work station and pulls out a neck strip. He uses Sanek, the leaders in neck strips. They catch loose hair and absorb perspiration and drips. Neck protection is required by state law because it prevents soiled hair-cutting capes from touching the customer's skin, which really is gross. John is standing behind Wayne with his neck strip. Wayne wants to know what the fuck John is doing, and John says he is giving Wayne a haircut, and Wayne says he does not want a haircut, and John says he thought Wayne said he thought he was going to want a haircut today, and Wayne says now he does not, so John crumples up the neck strip and disposes of it properly. He tells John to check out the picture of Ryan Newman. John leans over and checks it out. Ryan Newman is behind the wheel of his No.12 Dodge and leaning out. Wayne says he got 3rd at the 300 in Martinsville and says that it says that his favorite food is pizza. John says he loves pizza, too. Wayne says everybody does. John asks Wayne if he likes Papa John's more or Domino's more. Wayne tells John which one he likes more and John says he likes that one more, too, and says that he likes the other one, too, but that he likes the other one more. They talk about toppings. Wayne says his day sucked. John says he had a good day. He says he did a temple fade and a high and tight today. John says now he has cut eight people's hair since he opened for business. Wayne wants to know how long he is going to count for, and John says he does not know. Maybe until he loses count. Then John turns off the TV. He says he needs to get going because his mom is making burritos tonight. Wayne says to take a ride with him for a second. John says he cannot because his mom is making burritos tonight. He says he hopes she bought the black bean and shredded beef kind, which is his favorite kind. Wayne says it will only take five minutes, and John asks what will. Wayne says he wants to show him something, and John asks what he wants to show him. Wayne tells John that he just has to show him and that it will only take ten minutes. John says because after they eat they are going to finish playing Trouble. That is the one classic race-ahead, bump-back game with the Pop-o-Matic dice roller. They each play with two colors because it is more fun and hard that way. He makes sure the door is locked. It is. He stands and looks at his new barber pole and watches it spin around and around. Then Wayne honks so he gets in the car and then a little later turns around to see what the noise is. He tells Wayne he first thought it was coming from his speakers. Wayne says his radio is busted, and John says he thought he got it fixed already, and Wayne says he did, but it busted again. John asks Wayne since when he has a dog. Wayne says he just got it. John asks Wayne if it bites, and Wayne says it does not bite, so John reaches back and pets it. He wants to know its name. Wayne says Skipper. John says that that is a neat name. John says it is a dachshund. Dachshunds do not have strong doggy odors and are good companions for young and old. They are prone to disc problems. John asks Wayne what they are doing all the way down by the river for. Wayne says to just get out and he will show him. John says okay. He is amenable and really curious now. Wayne and John get out of the car. John steps in some mud. He says shoot. One of the car wheels is in the mud. Wayne opens the back door for Skipper. Skipper does not want to jump out at first. It is a long way down for Skipper. But Skipper finally jumps out. Wayne tells him that he is a good boy. You can tell that Wayne likes Skipper, and Skipper seems happy to see Wayne again, too. John says to look at all the clouds. He says he thought it was sunny just a second ago and wipes his shoe off on the road and leaves a mud streak on the road. Wayne gets out the outdoor power equipment out of the trunk. Then him and Skipper lead the way. They cut through a field that also has some trees in it. Skipper has a difficult time jumping through the field. He does not give up, though. Skipper is excited. John is, too. He is dying to know where they are going. Then his one shoe almost comes off in some more mud. John is having problems with the mud today. Wayne stops, and then Skipper stops, and then John catches up to Wayne and Skipper and stops, too. Wayne tests out the chainsaw on a branch. It was engineered with safety in mind. Skipper is a little scared because of the noise. Wayne tells Skipper not to be scared. Skipper does not hear Wayne because of the noise. Skipper is so scared he runs around John's legs in tight circles. John kneels down in the grass to pet Skipper. That is when he realizes he forgot to take his smock off. He laughs about it. He guesses he just loves being a barber. He tells Wayne to look and how that he forgot to take his smock off. John can feel his one knee getting wet in the grass. There is a light drizzle. Wayne tells John to cut his foot off for him. John's eyes get real big. He gives this sort of smile. He wants to know what is going on. Wayne tells John to put it in this bag and to bring it to this address and to put it in the mailbox. John hears the words, but it is like they do not register. Wayne gives John a plastic bag and a piece of paper with an address on it. John can tell it really is Wayne's handwriting. Wayne gets Skipper to come to him. Skipper is shaking with fear. Wayne tells John to take it. He means the chainsaw. He says he is going to lie down and then for John to do it. He has to scream all this because of the chainsaw. John says no way. He sticks his hand out to emphasize no. The chainsaw goes right through four of his fingers. It goes through them like butter. Wayne hardly notices, but John does right away. He does not scream at first because it is such a shock. It is the biggest shock of his life. John just stares at his hand. Skipper senses danger and wiggles free of Wayne. First he dashes one way, then he dashes the other way. Skipper is not sure which way he should go. Then he dashes back the same way they came from. He runs as fast as his little legs will carry him. He skids out when he reaches the road. Skipper turns left and runs down the road. John's four fingers are lying in the grass. One finger is in a little puddle. It almost does not even look like a finger the way it is lying there under water. It is the ring finger. Blood is getting all over John's smock. He is fortunate to still have his thumb. Wayne says shit. He drops the chainsaw. The motor cuts automatically, which is just one of this model's safety features. Then John starts to scream. He screams real loud. He screams about his hand. He is holding his hand with his other hand and falls over on his side. John's head almost rolls over in the same puddle where his finger is. Wayne asks John if he is all right. John is unable to answer the question. Wayne says that John is going to be all right. He says they just have to get to the hospital.

He tries to get John up. It is hard because John is all doubled-up. Wayne has to pull and lift and do everything he can to get him up. He gathers John's fingers, too. But he overlooks one. Wayne helps John to the car. John is starting to turn white. Wayne tells him not to faint. Then one of John's fingers squirts out of his hand. John says he cannot keep going. Wayne says he has to. Wayne says that John has to be strong. They really start to bond. They slip and fall. Then they both get up. John finally loses that one shoe. Wayne says they are almost there. The drizzle has really started to rain. Wayne gets John into the back seat of the car. John curls up on the back seat. He is bleeding everywhere, but Wayne only has vinyl seating. The car gets stuck in the mud. Wayne puts the car in reverse. Then he puts it in forward again. Then he puts it in reverse again. Wayne has not been stuck in the mud in years. Then Wayne gets the car out of the mud. He does a nice three-point turn, then flies down the road. He passes Skipper right up. Skipper has stopped running. Wayne asks John how he is doing back there. John asks Wayne to drive faster. Wayne says he is. He searches for Skipper in his rearview mirror. Wayne turns right, and the traffic gets heavier. Wayne flashes his lights and honks his horn. He waves his arm out of the window for people to pull over. It gets drenched because it is raining hard. Most of the cars pull over. But some of the cars do not always get what is going on. Wayne does his best, but it is still stop-and-go because of a lane closing. John wants to know when they are finally going to get there. Wayne says they are just now passing Frozen Frank's. Their Swirls are so thick they can be turned upside-down. Then Wayne swipes into a No Parking pole by the emergency entrance. Medical personnel come rushing out in white uniforms. It has stopped raining. It was one of those short summer showers. They get John out of the car. He goes blank. The next thing John knows his eyes start to open. His mom is right there next to his bed. She has a tissue in her hands. She is praying that he is going to be all right. John is her son. That means a lot to her. John sees lots of blurry things. Nothing is clear. It looks like there are flowers next to his bed. John has never received flowers before. John's mom lays a hand on John's forehead. She says John. There are tears in her eyes. John tries to focus. He does not know where he is yet. He does not know what happened yet. He asks her what she is watching. His voice is distant and weak. John's mom turns and looks up at the TV mounted on the wall. Then she turns back to John. She says The Price Is Right.

The Grumbler

Jen asks Mike what the doctor said. Mike tells her what he said. She says that Mike has to be kidding or the doctor has to be kidding. He says he is not. She asks him if he really has acne and sounds incredulous. Mike says if that is what he said he said or how many more times is he supposed to say it. Mike is irritable, which is understandable and comprehendible. Mike is an adult. The surprising acne is only on his forehead, and not on his nose, chin, and cheeks, too, but only on his forehead, which is good. He does not have any acne on his shoulders or back, where they are usually big, gross, and hidden. Jen tells Mike not to be snippish to her about it, that she cannot do anything about it, that he can use some of her cover-up for it, and finally gets the new jar of mayo open. Jen puts it down on the table and asks him if her hair looks okay. Mike says it looks just fine. He says it in a way that says that he did not even notice it or does not even care about it or that it does not even matter. That is what gets Jen mad, that kind of disregard. She says so. Mike apologizes. He says that her new taint or tone does look good, but that it is just that it is not like they are going to a party or the mall where everyone is going to see them. That is what gets Jen mad again, that kind of she does not know what. She leaves the kitchen to go down to the basement to get some more buns out of the freezer and brings them back up and warms up three in the micro because they are frozen and because that is how many she thinks they will probably end up still needing and comes back over to the table and sits down. Mike asks Zack for the second-to-last time to put down the game and to just watch the game. Zack and Brandy are also at the table. They have all been huge Padre fans ever since they went to California on vacation and to San Diego with its mild Mediterranean climate, and where Mike accidentally nicked a guy on a bike. It ruined the guy's bike, but it did not ruin their vacation, only about one hour. The Nats are whipping the Padres. Peavy just does not feel great and does not have great velocity, even though he keeps grinding and reaching down. The Nats jumped to a six-run lead in the first inning. Zack is afraid it will be 54 zip by the time the game is over. Mike says that that is no reason to give up on them and that you do not just give up on people when they are down. You root more. Then Mike tells Zack that if he does not put down his game, he might just turn off the game as well, in which case there will not be any games whatsoever for the rest of lunch. Jen leans over to see how much is left in Zack's game. She tells him to go ahead and finish it and then to turn it off. That is an agreement everybody finally agrees with and can live with. Mike stares over at Zack. He estimates that they have about the same number of pimples, but that maybe he has a few less, which he hopes. Mike simply refuses to entertain the notion that the hair follicles under his skin are clogging up. It does not make sense. It does not add up. Mike has frequently heard about adult women experiencing mild or even moderate acne due to pregnancy, menstrual cycles, or use of the pill, but Mike is just a guy. He keeps telling his forehead in the mirror to come on or to come off it. He makes this face and clenches his fingers. He asks Brandy why she is not eating her burger. He asks her if she does not like it, and whether it is undercooked or overcooked. He says there is almost no way it can be overcooked because he almost never overcooks. Mike only overcooked that one time when the riding mower slipped out of gear after he hopped off it to flip the burgers and started heading for the neighbor's trampoline with safety enclosure. Brandy does not answer him because she does not hear him because she is listening to music. Zack wants to know how come Brandy gets to listen to music and he does not get to play his game. Jen says something like hoot except without the t real loud and deep because Mike Cameron gets a stand-up double. Mike says Zack, then motions to Brandy with his finger to take off her music. Brandy understands the motion and is real cool about it. She takes off her music and does not complain or huff about it. That makes Mike relax inwardly because Zack now has nothing to base his argument on. It makes him want to say hoot without the t himself about himself. Mike encourages Brandy to eat some of her burger. He says she can even just eat half of it. Brandy says she is not hungry. Mike looks at his watch. He grants that it is earlier than normal for lunch, but that with everything going on he did not know how to fit everything in. Brandy tells him it is okay and not to worry about it. Mike says thanks. He says that it is just that she looks so thin and that he does not want her to get too thin. Brandy tells him that she does not have anorexia or is not too thin or bulimia. Jen says that nobody is saying that anybody has anything right when Josh Bard smacks a single which brings in Mike Cameron. The whole family cheers and remembers how they went to see them in San Diego where they lost. Mike drums the table and says that it is about time they get going to the funeral parlor and asks who wants to go see Grandpa. Brandy answers first and says she is not going because she is going over to Cassy's to research colleges. Brandy and Cassy are inseparable. They want to go to college together. Mike says that that is alright and okay, and that that is fine. He tells her to reach for the stars and to also find out as much as she possibly can about financial aid. He asks Zack what his plans are and calls him buddy. Zack says that he does not know yet and that he was thinking of maybe about staying home and working some more on his school project. Jen asks him if he has been learning a lot about volcanoes. Zack says that he has been learning gobs and tells her how hot the magma chamber can get in degrees Celsius. Mike says jeez and that you could fry an egg on that in no time. Jen makes sure that Mount St. Helen's was a volcano. Mike says he is pretty sure it was. Zack confirms and states that it is an active stratovolcano. Mike says that he sees a problem, the problem being that they are going to be gone for a while and that he does not really want Zack home alone for all that long. Then Mike does some thinking. He says he has an idea. Mike asks Brandy if it would be possible for Cassy to come there and to do their research there on their computer. He says that in that way Zack would not be home all by himself. Brandy says that that should not be a problem at all. She calls Cassy and they talk, and then Brandy says to hold on a second, and then she says that she will still need a car to pick up Cassy because Cassy does not have a car today, which was why she was going to go over there today in the first place. Mike says that that will be fine, but that he would still prefer her to take the old one if that would be fine, and it is. Brandy gets the keys out of the drawer where the keys always are. Sometimes they get all tangled up with the other things in the drawer's tray organizer which promises to compartmentalize your desk drawers. They really get tangled up with the paper clips and rubber bands. Today they do not at all. She says good-bye to everybody and tells Zack that she will be back in about twenty-five minutes and that she needs the computer all afternoon. Zack says he knows, and Mike tells Brandy to keep her phone on, and Brandy says she knows and always does and leaves, and Mike looks at his watch again and asks Jen if she is ready to leave, and Jen asks Mike if he is going to wear that shirt. Mike looks down at his shirt and wants to know what is wrong with his shirt. Jen says that it looks sloppy. Mike says it is his favorite shirt and that he loves this shirt. Since it is Zack's day off, he does not have to help his dad clear the table while Jen freshens up. Mike tells Zack to just keep on rooting, and Zack says ok and that he will. Mike says to send him a message on how the game ends up, and

Zack says ok and that he will. Mike wants to know if Zack is even listening to him, and Zack says yeah, and Mike says good. He puts everything back away where Jen likes to have it and wipes the table crumbs onto the floor and scatters them around with his shoe when the coast is clear. Zack says to watch out because he is dancing or something in front of the TV. Mike apologizes, and Mike and Jen leave. Before they leave, Jen gives Zack a kiss, and Mike tells Zack to keep his phone on and to call them in case his volcano starts lavagating their house, and Zack says that that is not a word. Mike and Jen are in the car. She wants to hear more about the acne. Mike puts on his blinker as he approaches the intersection and says that if it is alright with her he would rather not talk about it. Mike just wants to leave his zits out of it. Jen says she understands, but that they are right in the middle of his forehead. Mike agrees on that and tries to look at himself in the rearview mirror. Then he says that he just wants to concentrate on today. Jen rests her hand for a moment on Mike's leg, who is driving, and says she understands. But then right after that she says that she does not understand what could have caused it and wonders if the doctor said what could have caused it. Mike says stress and hates when he does not hit the first light because it stays red forever. Mike says the doctor did say something else about it, but that he did not catch all of it. Jen asks why he did not just re-ask if he did not catch all of it. Mike says he does not know. Mike says because he just wanted to get a prescription and get out of there because he had other fucking things on his mind, which Jen understands and puts her hand back on his leg for a moment. Jen stares out the window at the new car wash that just went up and where the high school cheerleaders are out jumping away and having a ball with their signs that say Car Wash. They want to raise money for the high school by washing your car. Jen sometimes hates the bodies those little bitches have, but Mike rarely if ever does. Mike says if he had known about the fundraiser he would not have washed his car yesterday after getting home after work and before making dinner. He can imagine sitting there with his seatbelt on as they bend over and reach over with the big F on the front of their uniforms and sponge down his windshield. They pass the IGA. Mike tells Jen to remind him to stop at the IGA on the way home. He says they need to pick up a few things. Jen asks what they need, and Mike tells her that they need more peaches for one thing. Jen says she thought he just bought some peaches. Mike says he did, but that Zack always devours them all on the first day, and that he does not know what to do about it. He asks if Jen does, and Jen does not. They think about a limit of two peaches per day. Then Jen asks what else. Mike says bagels, and Jen goes bagels? She asks Mike who eats bagels in the house. Mike says he kind of does and that is why he thought he would pick some bagels up and see how he likes them. He says it might be harder to make a sandwich out of them because of the hole in the middle, but that he is in the mood for a change and for something new and is going to try them out for a change. Mike says a guy at work brings them to work and that they traded sandwiches once last week and that he thought it was pretty dang good. Jen asks who he traded with, and Mike says someone she does not know. Jen still wants to know who. Mike says Nils from over in auditing. Jen says that she never heard him mention him before, and Mike says that is just what he just said. Jen asks what his first name is. Mike says that that is his first name because he is Scandinavian or Norwegian or something. Then Mike signals and turns into the funeral home. He says it is right where the Wet Willies Wild Waterslide used to be when he was growing up. Jen says she knew he was going to say that. It went under after a series of regrettable accidents. The parking lot is packed. It is Saturday afternoon. Mike circles around to try and find a spot and cannot believe that he cannot find a spot. Then he thinks he sees one, but it turns out to be a small car. Mike wonders to Jen if they should get a hybrid next, even though the space that turned out to be a small car is not one. Jen says she does not know. Mike says it is unbelievable. He says he remembers them saying how that all the halls were booked and how that his dad got the last one, but that he still did not expect anything like this. Mike says they should have gotten here earlier to beat the rush. He sees the clock on the dashboard and says he still has some viewing time. Mike tells Jen that he knows what he is going to do, and Jen asks what. Mike starts telling Jen that he is going to park over at the shed store that sells nothing but sheds, and that they will just cut through the lot when his cell rings. It is Zack. Mike says hey buddy. Jen can hear Zack yelling from the passenger seat. Mike says whoah, whoah, and to calm down. He says to repeat what he said because he did not understand a thing he said. Jen wants to know what is going on. Mike gives her this look and says that that is what he is trying to find out. He listens to what Zack says and then asks him if he has tried turning it off, and Zack says about a million times already. Mike tells him to try turning it off again. Jen is dying to know what Zack is trying to turn off. So many different gadgets and appliances come to mind that it is nearly impossible for Jen to guess which one. Mike tells her that Zack says the grumbler will not shut off. Mike asks him if it shut off now. Zack says no. Mike tells him to hold the receiver over the drain. He wants to try and diagnose the problem over the phone. Zack does, but the disposal sounds normal to Mike. Mike asks Zack what he put down the drain, but Zack is still holding the phone over the drain and does not hear him. Mike yells Zack a couple of times to get Zack back on the phone. Zack says that he told him that it was broke. Mike tells him to say broken. He asks him what he put down the drain. Zack says a banana peel. Jen asks Mike what it was, and Mike tells her a banana peel. Mike says that banana peels belong in the trash from now on, and Zack says okay, and Mike tells Jen that he said okay. Mike tells Zack to just not use the sink until they get back. Jen tells Mike to tell Zack not to stick his hand down the drain. Mike says duh to Jen. Jen mouths something

The Grumbler

to Mike that looks like fuck you or asshole. Zack wants to know duh what. Mike denies that he said duh, but Zack says that he heard him say duh. Mike says he said uh, as in uh he was thinking what to do next. Mike tells him to just forget it and tells him to open up the cabinet under the sink and try pushing the grumbler's red reset button. Jen yells that Zack is not to touch the grumbler. Mike says that he is only going to touch the outside of the grumbler. Somebody honks behind Mike. Mike gives an apologetic wave and starts circling the parking lot again. He tells Zack to hang on a second. Brandy calls her mom to say that Zack is being so loud and that they cannot research colleges when he is being so loud. Jen asks her to go into the kitchen to help her brother with the garbage disposal. Mike is able to pull enough over to the side to let the car behind him squeeze by. Mike again waves friendily to the other guy, and the other guy does the same without any trace of road rage. The whole family conferences on how they are going to resolve the problem with the grumbler. They have a family plan from Verizon so the calls are not costing anybody anything. Verizon is so awesome. Everybody hangs up, and Mike drops Jen off back home. He tells Jen that there is also an Allen wrench in the coffee can under the sink. He says that it fits into the bottom of the grumbler and that it can sometimes break loose the blades if the blades are jammed. Mike says if all else fails to turn off the electricity. Jen wants to know what they are supposed to do in the dark. Mike says that it is not dark and that it is the middle of the day. He says to open a drape. Mike says that that Allan wrench that he was just talking about that came with the grumbler is half-assed. He says that it might round over right away, but that there is a hex on both ends and so to try the other end, too. Jen says she is not getting under the sink. She says that if anything she is going to call a plumber. Mike asks her if she has any clue what a plumber costs on the weekend and then tells her how much since she does not. She gets out and closes the door, and Mike drives back to the funeral parlor, which is playing soft music when he walks in. Mike recognizes the song after only a few bars and before his eyes adjust to the dim lighting. When they do, there is a man standing right there in front of him. He asks him what party he belongs to and then escorts him there and opens the door for him. Mike walks in and spots his dad right away lying up in front. Mike goes up there. He says he is sorry he is late, but says he will not believe what all happened today. Mike tells his dad the whole rat race, starting with his acne. He says if it is not one thing, it is another. He tells him about the AVP job he is up for and says that he has to remember to tell Jen about it and then tells him how Jen was all against him wearing this shirt, but that it is his favorite one. He says he knows his dad has to remember it because he always wears it. Mike tells him it is a pretty nice hall or room and says it is set at a pretty comfortable temp. Mike turns back around and estimates how many chairs there are. He tells his dad he will be right back and goes and gets a chair. He tells his dad that even if the grumbler does give up the ghost, that the thing lasted him almost thirteen years, but that he thinks it is the switch and not the grumbler per se. He tells his dad that the chairs may look pretty nice, but that they are pretty uncomfortable. Then Mike just sits there for a while and relaxes. Then that same guy from before comes in. He nods his head and gestures slightly to his watch. Mike nods his head, and the man exits. Mike relaxes a second more before putting his hands on his knees and saying well. He tells his dad he better get going. He tells his dad he will be back by tomorrow for the funeral. He says then he will bring him out to Mom. He says Mom will be happy. He says everybody knows how much Mom loves company.

An Emu Is Like an Ostrich

Donna gets in her mom's lane because her mom gets an employee discount. Donna's mom is real good with a checkout scanner. She is real fast. She plays an integral role in providing a great customer experience. She is knowledgeable of the layout of the store. She knows the merchandise inside and out. Donna's mom is accurate and comfortable with math and currency. They say hi. Donna's mom checks her out. It is back-to-school time. There is a ton of crud in her cart. There is a pack of 12 high-quality pens with anti-pushback points that ensure dependable writing. Donna bought glue sticks with this gorilla on them that the girls will go ape over. The girls love ground-dwelling, predominantly herbivorous primates. Donna's cart is like avalanche city. Crud keeps falling all over. Her mom's scanner is beeping like mad. It is like pinball machine city. The self-stick framed bulletin boards are unique and durable. Their whole surface is sticky so tape, pins, and tacks are not required. That saves you time and hassle. Pins are the real hassle. Donna's mom asks Donna how they are doing. Donna tells her. Then come the backpacks. Her mom says they are selling a lot of those or these, a lot of backpacks. Donna says how long and hard she looked and thought before picking the ones she finally picked. Donna has gone with the ones with Ergonomic Back System. You may be familiar with Ergonomic Back System as EBS. It was either between EBS or Big Student. Big Student has a 2200 cubic inch capacity. That makes Big Student bigger, but Big

Student does not have EBS. That was the whole problem right there. But Big Student has a front zippered organizer pocket. It has two exterior supplement pockets for school supplies. That was the whole dilemma right there. But then Donna thought of her girls' backs. Her girls' backs are important to her. That was the kicker right there. That was the bottom line right there. That is what she is going to tell Jim, too. She hates when Jim thinks she made the wrong decision and then gets all whatever about it. Donna's mom keeps checking out more crud. Then finally that is all the crud, which was like a ton of crud, and her mom goes on break, and her and her mom sit down in the snack area right there and have a cheesy pretzel. Donna's mom gets to get free cheesy pretzels. She could get ten if she wants. She could get twelve. One of the girls once got four after doing five straight hours in the express lane. They sit there eating their cheesy pretzels and getting cheese everywhere. It oozes right off no matter how fast you scarf it down. You might as well not even try is what the girls say. The best is to just let it ooze off and forget about it and cut your losses. It is not like you had to pay for it. Her and her mom need like 500 of these thin napkins you get with it. They do not absorb crud. She asks her mom if she can take some home with her for her girls' gerbils. Fuzzy and Wuzzy love chewing up paper products. You can put a toilet paper roll in their cage, and it is like chomp city. It is gone. It goes to make their bedding they cuddle up in. Her mom gets up and brings her back a whole stack. Donna says how she is worried because Pammy starts middle school on Monday. Pammy is not very coordinated and wears glasses. Donna does not want Pammy to get all picked on by the bigger kids. She hopes Pammy can get the combination right on her locker. She finally finishes her cheesy pretzel and says how she does not see how you can eat four cheesy pretzels. Her mom says how that is why they say you can eat as much as you want because they know you cannot. Then Donna's mom pulls something out of the front pouch of her uniform vest thing.

It is a long and silvery thing. Donna asks her mom what it is. The pretty, heart-shaped locket has a minuscule dent in it and does not open. You cannot even see the dent. You would never even guess it was there. That is how come her mom got it. The girls sometimes get damaged goods for free or for like 50 cents. Sometimes they fight or argue over it or them. Her mom shows it to Donna. The rope chain is 24 inches in length and draped between her mom's fingers. She made real sure she got all the cheese off her fingers first. The locket part of the locket is tri-color. It has a classic floral design. Donna says how pretty it is and how there is no way you can see the dent. She says her mom should try it on. Her mom asks if she should really try it on right there. Donna says frick yeah and to go for it. She tries it on. Donna says it looks real good. That makes her mom feel real good. Her mom says she is thinking of asking Ernie if Ernie wants to give it to her while on their trip. She calls him Ern when they are alone but says Ernie with everybody else. His full name is probably Ernest. She says how the only thing Donna's daddy ever got her was a black eye. She says how Ernie cannot be buying things for her with his wife around. Donna asks her mom what trip she is talking about and that she does not know anything about a trip. Donna's mom asks Donna if she did not tell her about the trip. Donna says she does not know crud about a trip. Donna's mom says she must have forgot, and that they are going to the Cliffs. Donna looks pretty surprised when her mom says that about the Cliffs. She says how the Cliffs seem pretty far away. Donna's mom says how Ernie loves driving and never gets lost. Donna says how even if you do not get lost, you can hardly get to the Cliffs and back in one day. It is mainly all two-lane roads to the Cliffs. Plus there are all these curves that make you car-sick if you sit in the back. Donna's mom says how they will be gone two days. Donna is like what the frick. She wants to know what they are going to be doing at the Cliffs for two days. She says how you can see the Cliffs in like half an hour. At the Cliffs you basically just stand around and look around and then drive back. They are very pretty. Donna's mom says how they are not too old to figure out what to do for two days. She asks Donna to come by and feed the cat and water her cactuses. Donna's mom has this huge cactus collection. Donna asks her mom if she has enough cat food or if she should go back and get some cat food since she is already here. You can get everything here. Donna's mom says she has enough. She says to give the cat turkey & giblets the first day and salmon the second day. Donna says okay and asks her mom what is going to happen if Ernie's wife ends up getting better. Donna's mom says she ain't going to get better and takes off the locket and puts the locket back in that front pouch thing. She has to get back to work and gets up. Something goes crunch. Her and Donna look down. But it was just some popcorn she stepped on. It blends right in with the tiles. You cannot even see it. Donna gets up too. She has to go and pick up the girls from animal camp. She says how they were supposed to be petting an emu today. It is like an ostrich.

Home Theater

The doorbell rings. Terry does not hear the doorbell because of the blender. It is on. It has a powerful motor which takes on large batches. It whirls through thick batters. It is going to be a Moist Supreme Classic Yellow cake with Funfetti frosting. Funfetti is like confetti you eat in the frosting. It is fun. It is just the right touch for special occasions. Her husband Terry does hear the doorbell. That is going to be a problem. Both their names are Terry. It was a source of amusement at one point in time a long time ago. The one Terry has a mustache. That might help keep them apart. To change their names would only distort reality since Terry is their names. Terry hears the doorbell, but it does not look like he does. Terry keeps sitting there jousting on the coffee table. One medieval knight and his horse is clad in red, and the other one and his horse is clad in black. The black one is the meaner one. He has this grimace on his face. They are rendered in stunning detail and nontoxic paint. The trio of foot soldiers are battle-ready. Only the flail-bearing foot soldier is not. He is tipped over on a magazine article Terry was reading about how increasing vitamin D can make a difference. Imagine being whacked by a flail. The catapult works. Terry one time put the little capiz balls that Terry collects when she was not looking into the catapult and tried to hit the thing up on the mantelpiece that says Always in heavy aluminum letters. Always can get to be a long time. Always can take forever. Today makes forty years. The jousters came included with a quintain. The foot soldier with the hauberk gets jousted in the back. He did not have a chance. He was looking off at the Kilim pillow which mingles suavely in any living area. The batter does not have any lumps because the blender reaches every corner of the bowl. Terry turns off the blender with a ten-speed control and sleek design. She does not know who is going to eat it. Terry does not like anything she ever makes, and she has to watch her diabetes, and deep down she knows no one is coming. She might feed it to the birds in her back yard. They are her feathered friends. Companionship is important. Terry would love to have a birdbath. She could watch them take a bath and splash in the water. Now Terry hears the doorbell because Chad rang it again. He is the one who rang it the first time. Terry wonders if maybe her son has flown in after all and brought her grandkids but not his wife. That would brighten her day and her life. Terry wipes her hands on the dish towel with the grapes on it. The grapes looked so ripe and juicy when it was new. Terry tells herself not to get her hopes up, but since they are all she has. She checks her hair in the mirror by the door. It says I love me. The doorknob is wobbly. Anybody could break in and club them to death. Chad says he is there for the pest control. Terry says that the termite inspection is scheduled for next week. She tells him what today is and goes on and on about it and her son. Chad says he does not know nothing about all that. He says he is just the termite guy and that all he knows is what it says here on his clipboard. He turns it around to show Terry. It is one of those brown clipboards. It has the names, addresses, and dates of all his appointments on it. Terry sees her name, or Terry's name, and today's date on it. Terry overhears his name and wonders what the hell the problem is. Terry throws a foot soldier against the wall since his grandsons are never going to come and play with them. First it whizzes through the air, then it ricochets off one wall and into another wall, and then it just lands on the carpet. The foot soldier probably does not even know what wall-to-wall carpet is since they did not have it back when the likes of him ruled the forests. Terry's wife has that confused look on her face that he hates. He hates it on the inside without you being able to tell on the outside. Terry asks how he may help Chad. Chad responds by saying he is there for termite treatment. It is a job for professionals. Homeowners should not just wake up one morning and try it on their own. He has a large assortment of equipment in his white utility van. There are masonry drills, pumps, large-capacity tanks, soil treatment rods, and several gallons of liquid pesticide in his van. Chad wears a mask when spraying. Terry tries telling Terry that Chad cannot come now. Terry wants to know why not. Then Terry and Terry stare at each other for maybe two seconds, which is more than enough. Resentment can totally snowball over the course of forty years. Terry goes back into the kitchen. She misses her involvement with Camp Lutherwood. She was treasurer. She misses Jayne's BBQs and playing chuck-it with Smokey and Good Guy Bob who could fix anything and went around saying he could even repair a cloudy day. It had to close after what happened with Justin who managed the climbing and ropes course when the Feds came and got him down out of the tree. Justin's favorite verse had always been Matthew 28:18-19. All authority in heaven and on earth has been given to me. People interpreted it differently after what happened. Justin got a big head and ruined it for everybody. Terry hates Justin as she pours the batter into a cake pan and puts the cake in the oven. Terry follows Chad out to his white utility van. Chad says how spring is swarmer season all right and opens up the back of his white utility van. He says you cannot blame them. He says that we all like warm weather, us and the termites. Terry says it is a nice day out as an aerial advertisement for Saga Insurance flies by. Saga Insurance wants to establish itself in town, but it will never make inroads against Richard's Allstate. Richard has half the town over-protected. People have come to trust him. Chad puts down a jug of Prevail on the driveway. It could use repaving, but Terry did not fall for the driveway paving scam that made its way across the state last summer. Terry says that the jug looks pretty dangerous. Chad says toxic shit. He laughs. Terry sees his teeth are brown and missing. Chad tells Terry that any given termite colony has three castes because it is part of his job. The workers, the soldiers, and the reproductives are the three castes. Chad is stuffing his pant leg down into his rubber boots. Terry says he wants to ask Chad something. Chad tells him to go for it. Terry wants to know if Chad knows what it is like to be in charge of 1.7 million square feet of cleanable flooring in over 28 units, or individual buildings, and then to watch a bunch of arrogant young punks walk across them with perfect disregard day after day, year after year. Chad finally gets his second pant leg stuffed in his other rubber boot and asks Terry if he works over at the college or something. Terry says for almost thirty goddamn years real slow. Chad says no shit. He says because his cousin works over there at the steam plant and just loves it over there at the steam plant. Then he asks Terry where he can plug in his Hilti, and they never get back to discussing Terry's discontent. The first thing Chad is going to do is drill the foundation, he says. It is the first thing you do. It can get kind of loud. He asks Terry if he has a dog before opening the gate to the back yard. Then Chad opens the gate to the back yard and goes into the back yard. Terry stays out in the front yard. He wonders how long that plane is going to be circling around for. He picks up a little stone and tosses it up onto his roof. It goes bouncing back down and lands in the gutter. He does that for a while. It is like a game. She sees Chad walk by the sink window. Her Dobie is floating in the mixing bowl. The great thing about her cleaning pad is how it scours without scratching. The phone rings, and there she goes, getting her hopes up again. Her hopes are really going up and down today. It is Terry's sister. She wants to update her about Earl. They have him scheduled for a cholecystectomy after all. He will be able to go home the same day. Outpatient surgery is the way to go. People can convalesce in the comfort of their own homes. Earl is of Irish descent, likes to sit next to the fire and tell stories, and just retired. It has been one thing after another since he retired. First it was that freaky ingrown toenail and now it is stones. Terry's sister worries about what tomorrow might bring. Terry says it is hard to hear half of what she is saying because the termite guy is drilling. Terry's sister says that she did not realize that they had termites. Terry says that she did not either. She says how that Terry found them flying around the basement window one day and first thought they were ants. Terry does not know what he always does down in the basement to begin with. Terry is always going and staying down there. Terry's sister says that she did not realize that termites flew or that they looked like ants. She says that tonight she is going out with Pat, Earl's sister, to see Pat's son in Oklahoma! in the school play. Her son is the one the family is not so sure about. He is playing Will Parker, but some people behind his back have said he would make a good Laurey. People can be mean and yet right at the same time. It is opening night. They hang up. Terry takes the cake out of the oven which looks golden brown. She runs upstairs and locks herself in the bathroom. They have one of those old tubs with the feet that look romantic but are hard to clean. It is not like Chad grew up wanting to be a termite inspector. It is more like something you just become or turn into without actually striving for. It just happens to be the job you get. It has taught him something fundamental about life. How that you can run, but you cannot not hide. It is a fundamental concept that can make you paranoid if you take it too far. He has found the long arm of the Lord, unless it found him first. Chad has been meth-free for coming up on three years. The only time he missed his Narcotics Anonymous meeting was because of an occupational accident involving his respiratory system. Termite management actually begins with you, even if it ends with Chad. People do not realize the importance of eliminating all contact between wooden parts of a home's foundation and the soil. Firewood should never be stacked against the foundation, and mulch should never touch the house, but people never learn. That is good, because if they did, Chad would not have a job. Terry pretty much does next to nothing down there. He does not play ping-pong against the wall. If anything he sits in that musty old green armchair and reads some of his two-volume book about Caesar. It sounds like an interesting topic, given that the Roman leader had such a rich life. It seems to me, however, that it would do the both of them a lot better if they finally sat down and talked about their loss of love, alienation, and even mutual hatred. But who knows, maybe it is harder than you think after forty years. Especially for someone like me: married to a loving wife, three healthy kids, secure job, good school district, and no real pests to worry about. Except ants that one time. We went with baits and never heard from them again. Knock on wood. Ants get attracted to the baits to feed, but they are really eating Abamectin. Then they return to their nest, die, and keep on killing other ants because of the Abamectin. I strongly recommend baits. We are finally going to Florida this summer, the whole package deal. Benny, our oldest, has been after us about it for years. And now that Dotty's old enough. My bonus is covering the airfare, but my wife and I have not yet figured out how to do the window seats. One night I even said, guys, if you are going to keep on arguing about who gets a window seat, we are just going to all pile in the van and drive. You should have seen the look on their faces. Until Benny did the math, plugging in gas at $3.78 a gallon, and called my bluff. Then they all ganged up on me with their pillows. My wife made the popcorn, and we ended up camping out in the great room. Now that we have home theater, we often pop in Music of Nature. It is an incredible box set without any of the phony background music. It teaches our kids to appreciate how cool nature can be given the right conditions. The only qualm I have is that with five butt-kicking CDs, there is always some arguing about who wants to hear what track. The boys always want either Pig Frogs or Hoots and Howls, and Dotty Bayou because the alligators. Sometimes my wife and I are concerned about her fascination with solitary, territorial animals, but we are banking on it being only a phase. Like how the Nicker would not stop fondling himself for the longest time and then all of a sudden did. One night I almost even had to call decamp and send my troops to bed. I finally said it was going to be Mom's call or no call. Talk about bumming everybody out in a flash. Because they know Mom always picks Tropical Rain, which makes them tired and fall asleep a lot earlier than they want to. Which gives me and my wife a little snuggle time under a verdant canopy. Chad is back behind the wheel. He is ready to leave. He is not wearing shoes. Chad just changed into clean socks because that is what his doctor recommended. Chad finally went to see the doctor after his athlete's foot would not go away. Now he is supposed to change his socks at least once a day and let his feet air out between inspections. The doctor gave him a cream with something stronger than miconazole. The problem is being confined in rubber boots all day. They do not let his feet breathe. Terry comes out and asks Chad if he would like a piece of cake. Chad says you bet he would. He gets out of his utility van and walks in in his socks and says thanks. Terry says that Chad must be tired. Chad says he is. He says his job is a bone-buster, instead of saying a ball-breaker. He takes a load off. There is a glass of milk and everything. Terry asks Chad if he got all the termites. Chad says that the critters are rascals and that they will have to wait and see. Terry explains the frosting to Chad. He likes the cake and wolfs it down, and Terry gives him another piece of cake. They talk about the weather. Terry tells Chad that Tommy is about his height except that Tommy does not wear his hair as long in the back. Terry asks Chad if he has any children, and Chad says probably.

The Dark Continent

Rachel takes pictures of Gina. She takes gobs of them. Rachel and Gina are glad for digital cameras. They are the best. The first picture she takes of her is of her next to her fridge. Gina's one hand is resting on the freezer handle. She looks relaxed and rested and like she might be wanting to get some ice or other frozen item. Gina has a display of magnets on her fridge. They show up too small in the picture to tell what they are. Gina and Rachel are bummed about that. There is a 3-D magnet of a shopping cart that really looks full with jars and boxes and plastic and paper bags. Another magnet is a mini coffee mug that says World's Mommest Mom. Gina's daughter also gave her a matching real coffee mug to go with it. Gina likes coffee, so that was the perfect gift. The next picture of Gina is with her in front of her stove. One day Gina would love to have an electric stove because cleaning the grates are a pain. Sometimes she starts saving for one for a while, but then she needs the money for something else and starts saving for that instead. Off to one side in the picture you can see her red oven mitt. The thumb part has been turned away from the camera because it got burnt once and is black and melted. Gina and Rachel agreed that that would not look good and nice. In one picture the stove light is on, and in one it is not. They both look good. They do not know what one looks better. The kitchen theme was Rachel's idea. Rachel thought it would be an awesome idea. Rachel had other ideas, too. Outside next to the maple tree was one other idea. The problem with that idea is the rain. It is raining, or at least drizzling. That is the whole problem. Rachel has tons of ideas that are good. Rachel says how there is not a straight man alive out there not looking for a gal who can cook. Rachel says being good under the covers might get them, but being good in the kitchen will keep them. They laugh at that one. Rachel is the funny one. She is also the more outgoing one, the younger one, the thinner one, and the more attractive one. Rachel has a steady boyfriend. Gina loves casseroles.

    She has a pretty microwave that takes up a lot of counter space. Rachel says to emphasize your strong points. She says to hit them with your best shot. She says you only have the one shot. Rachel says how the picture is the most important element. Rachel says if the picture is not a grabber, then they are not going to click you. Rachel says that you have like barely one whole second to grab them. That disheartens Gina. That makes her want to stop and give up. That makes her want to forget the whole dang thing. That makes her want to try some other way or just not try at all. Rachel wants to know what other way. Gina just kind of sits or stands there. Rachel says she is waiting and listening. Gina says she does not know. Rachel says unmarried hunks do not go looking for babes in church basements. Gina laughs and agrees. But then Gina says she is not a grabber type person in terms of how looks go. Gina says she will not be able to reach out and grab anybody in like one second. Gina says she is not J Lo or whoever. But Rachel says she is not out to get Ben Affleck or whoever, or George Clooney or whoever. Rachel says to come on and to smile. Her digital camera has over seven megapixels. It is a good thing that Gina has a nice smile. When people come into the office, she greets them with a good smile that is natural. Gina loves her job where her and Rachel work and where Rachel does bookkeeping. They make commercial refrigeration. The office part is right off the factory part. You would think it would be real loud in the office part, but for whatever reason it is not.

    Rachel has Gina sit down at her kitchen table next to a loaf of white bread. The bread is not in the plastic bag. They took it out to make it look like it is homemade or something. Rachel tells Gina to put her arms up on the table and to pull down her sleeves for this one which are jammed up like always by her elbow. Gina does. Rachel says to smile. She says to say cheese. Gina does. But Rachel says that for some reason Gina has that crud-eating grin again. Gina says she is getting tired of smiling. Rachel says one more smile. She says she can do it. Gina does, and Rachel takes the picture. Then they look at the pictures in the view-finder thingy. They delete a lot of them. Gina has her eyes closed in some of them or else partially shut. That makes her look tired and retarded. Then Rachel asks Gina what she thinks of this one. Gina says which one and to let her see. She moves her head and view-finder thingy around until she sees the picture just right and not like a negative. Gina says she does not know and asks Rachel what she thinks. Rachel says she thinks it might be the grand-prize winner. Gina asks Rachel if that is what she really thinks. Rachel says that really is what she thinks. Gina says okay and that if that is what she thinks then that is fine with her.

    The computer and Internet is in the spare bedroom so that is where they get up and go to next. Gina's daughter sleeps in the spare bedroom whenever she comes and visits. The house has like two bedrooms. Gina's daughter lives kind of far away. They talk a lot on the phone on this special family rate they have. Gina's daughter is in nursing. Otherwise the spare bedroom is where Droopy has his bed. Gina loves her dog tons and the fact that she has a fenced-in back yard where Droopy can run around whenever he wants. Droopy sleeps a lot now. The funny thing is that Droopy does not sleep in this bed she got for him. Droopy just sleeps wherever. That is Droopy for you all the way. It is not an orthopedic dog bed. It is a microvelvet donut dog bed. It is very snuggly. Gina's desktop takes forever to get going. Even Rachel asks how long the thing is going to take. Rachel thinks it might be some kind of a virus. Gina says it is just an old clunker. Then it finally gets going. Gina already registered with the dating service like Rachel told her to. So that is already done. Gina logs in to her account. Gina goes by geniepie4724. The next thing is to create a profile. Gina leaves the city blank but types in the state she lives in and how tall she is and how old she is and provides her marital status and ethnicity. Gina is Caucasian and a real fast typist. For education she puts some college which is technically true. For occupation she puts what she is. Then there is the one question pertaining to body type. Gina looks down at her body type and then back up at the cursor. It is blinking and waiting patiently for her to type something. Gina asks Rachel what she should type. She asks if she should just leave it blank or put N/A or something. Rachel says to be who she is and proud of it. Rachel is lying on the bed and staring up at a big fat water stain on the ceiling. Gina says that that is easy for Rachel to say. Rachel goes to aerobics class twice a week. Gina could go with for a free trial if she wanted, but she always says no. She says she walks her dog. Gina asks if she should put overweight or maybe just chubby. Gina says chubby might sound better. She says it might sound less overweight. Rachel says how that sounds lame and that overweight is even lamer. Rachel says a profile has to be fun and stand out and something people will want to meet. Rachel says how Gina has to remember how her profile has to reflect how Gina really is in real life. Gina says that in real life she is overweight. Rachel says they just need to think of another word for not thin. Gina says there is no way she is going to put fat. She says there is no way. Rachel thinks and then asks Gina what she thinks about huggable. Gina does this snorty laugh she always does that is sort of her trademark at the office but that Rachel says she should try and not do on a first date. Gina asks Rachel if she really thinks they can put that. Rachel says she does, so she does.

Then comes the hardest part. The hardest part is the About Me part. That is the part where you have to actually write a whole paragraph about yourself. Gina turns around to look back at Rachel. She does not know what in the heck to say. Rachel says Gina should just pretend she is talking to her about herself. Gina says okay and turns back around and does not start typing. She looks at the monster mess on her desk and all the stuff on it. She finds a Bugle that is not crushed to smithereens and throws it away. Then Gina still does not know what to write and turns back around again. She says she is going to get dizzy with all this turning around and wonders if she should go get another chair for Rachel from the kitchen. Rachel rolls over on her side and props her head up on her hand. It is a waterbed. Gina would love to get rid of it, but her daughter loves to sleep on it when she visits. Gina loves her daughter. She misses her, too. She is happy for her, too. Nursing is a good profession. You always need nurses. Gina hopes her daughter will meet a nice man, maybe even a doctor, or a nurse since now men are nurses, too. Gina thinks her daughter is very pretty. It is like she does not want to acknowledge the weird thing about her nose. Gina and Rachel make a mental list of all the things Gina likes or does or likes to do. Then they say okay. Then Rachel says just to write how she loves animals and people and taking walks and going out and just staying home by a warm fire. Gina says to slow down so she can type all this stuff and that she does not have a fireplace. Rachel says she is not saying she herself has a fireplace. Then Rachel says to write how she loves to cook for the right person who knows how to appreciate a good hearty meal. Gina likes that a whole lot and says that that is true with a capital T for her because she says she hates slaving in a hot kitchen for like three hours or an hour and then serve something steamy and scrumptious and then people are like, oh, and leave half of it on the plate. Gina hates cooking for the garbage disposal, which is how she calls it. Rachel is not much in to cooking. She says to write that she loves giving attention, but also getting some back every once in a while. Gina types it and asks if she is done. Rachel says she is almost done. Rachel says she needs to put what she wants and wants to avoid and what she is looking for. Gina says that that is easy. Gina says she wants a male partner minus the head games. Gina says she is so sick of head games. She really gets riled up on the topic of head games. Head games are like mind games. Rachel says that that sounds great and to put that. Then Gina says she is done no matter what Rachel says she is and gets Rachel to get up and look everything over before she clicks save. Rachel looks everything over and says everything looks great. Then Gina takes a deep breath and clicks save. Then Gina and Rachel high-five. Then they go back to Home and search her profile. Then they see they forgot the picture because it says No Picture Available. They are so stupid. They do not see how they could have done that after all the pictures they took. So they go back and do that. Then they high-five again, and Rachel says go girl and things like that.

    Then Rachel suddenly says shh and to be quiet. Gina looks all concerned because Rachel looks all worried and asks her what. Rachel is surprised Gina does not hear it. Gina wants to know hear what. Rachel gets a big smile on her face on account of her big mouth and says she hears wedding bells. Gina slaps Rachel in a soft and friendly way on her shoulder. She says to cut it out. Rachel says Gina is going to look lovely in white or peach. Gina says she is not just going to go out and marry the first guy she meets. Gina knows Rachel is just kidding her. Gina says she might not actually get married at all again even if her church does not believe in cohabitation without marriage. Gina says she does not really know why she should after the first time. Rachel says she should precisely because of the first time to show she can do it. Gina says she knows she can do it as long as the butthole does not hit her. Gina says if Rachel wants to go to a wedding so bad she is the one who should go and get married. Rachel says they are going to get married, but that Chase wants to wait until next year. He wants to wait until things fall into place. Gina wants to know like what. Rachel says just stuff and that they should contact some dudes now that Gina has her profile up. Gina says she is not going to contact anybody. She says she is going to wait for somebody to contact her. Rachel wants to know what the eff and what is up with her. Gina says because she does not want to seem like some fat, desperate, over-the-hill, 47-year-old hag and that that is why. Rachel tells Gina to come off it and not to be a lame-butt. She says Gina is not going to look desperate. She says contacting people is what everybody joined in the first place for. Gina does not say anything at first and then she says still. She says she has been living without a man for 19 years just fine and that if she wants to she can do the same for another 19 easy. That means Gina would be 66.

Rachel says what about this guy and clicks on an older, slightly balding widower in his mid-50s who likes fishing, is Caucasian, and went to high school and who friends say is very affable. Gina does not even look at him. He is wearing one of those outdoors vests with a gazillion pockets. Gina says she does not want to spend her weekends visiting some guy's wife's grave. Rachel says that from the looks of the picture it looks like he spends his weekends at some body of water. Gina says she does not like fishing. Rachel says how that you do not have to hook live bait anymore and that waking up early and eating fish is healthy for you on account of the omega-3 fatty acids. She says water is real relaxing and makes some waves on the waterbed. Rachel is just trying to help. Rachel knows for a fact that Gina is not all that unbothered and cool with being alone. You can just kind of tell in lots of little ways, like how all she has or ever talks about is that dog. Gina tells Rachel to log off. Rachel says she thought they were going to flirt some and play the field some and get some dates. Gina says it sounds like Rachel is the one who wants to flirt some and play the field some, and then she goes and puts some food in Droopy's dish. Then her and Rachel go roller-skating.

The Dark Continent

Gina says bye to Droopy before they leave, but Droopy does not notice. His head is down in his red dish chomping away. Droopy loves his kibble. Gina finally found some that does not give him all that gas. She says it costs more, but it is way worth it. She says it was getting pretty bad there for a while. Gina would be like, Droopy, not again, and Droopy would look up at her with these sad eyes. Droopy would not have the faintest idea what she was talking about or referring to. Droopy is brown in color. Gina has been trying to get Droopy to drink more because of how important liquids are. The vet said it was his kidneys. The problem is that Droopy does not want to, and if Droopy does not want to, he is not about to. Droopy can be as stubborn as a mule. Gina worries about Droopy. Rachel says not to worry. She says animals instinctively know what they need. Gina says she knows because she has heard about that on the radio. But she also says she has always been a worrier. She says she is just like her mom was in that respect. Her mom was a worrier who smoked and died of a heart attack at the age of 62. They go out through the kitchen door in the back because the front door jams. Gina has literally not opened the front door for a long time.

They just opened up the new roller-skating rink in town. It is a real big deal for the town. There was a town cook-out and everything when it opened. Gina and Rachel went. They each had slushburgers. They were so messy and greasy you had to use triple paper plates and take a handful of napkins and even then they were messy and greasy. They were real good. They did not touch something there called cheeseslaw. It looked gross. They first thought it was normal coleslaw and were going to take some. Then they found out it was something called cheeseslaw. Gina got some slushburger down on her sweatshirt. It said Hug a nurse and heal better. It is the same one she has on today. It is her favorite one because her daughter is a nurse. The letters are squished together in the middle to look like they are getting hugged. Gina wears sweatshirts a lot. They are her thing. She wears them with the sleeves pushed up. That is her thing, too, even though she does not have a tattoo or tattoos on her forearm or forearms. Musical entertainment was provided at the cook-out by Half Moon Rising. Half Moon Rising is a remarkably versatile cover and wedding band specializing in country rock. They are an instant draw for your music venue. They play music that is easily programmed for many different events, like firefighter benefits. They have been on the radio. They played up on this flatbed stage thing. They asked the crowd if they were ready to country rock. Some of the people standing around said they were and raised their plastic cups and so they started playing. The roller-skating rink has created valuable temporary construction jobs and enriching part-time other jobs where you hand out skates in exchange for people's shoes. For this position you have to be able to see good in dim lighting conditions, enjoy listening to loud music, and not be afraid to tell young adults that beverages are not allowed on the rink. Her and Rachel have been wanting to go ever since it opened since they did not actually go skating at the grand-opening.

Now they are finally here and park right up by the entrance. The place looks deserted, but that is only because the kids have to be dropped off and picked back up by their moms. They are all still too young to drive. It is right next to the auto parts store and the biggest gas station in town. It is the perfect, convenient location. They sit down on these low wide benches covered in carpeting and put on their skates. Rachel cannot get one of her skates on. Gina says to loosen up the laces more. Gina knows all about roller skates because she used to always go roller skating. It was real big when she was young. Rachel never really went. It was much less big when she was young. Fads always seem to come in waves. Rachel is not so sure how good she will be. She says it is not the laces. She says it feels like there is something down in her skate. Rachel reaches down in and pulls out a wadded up sock. It has a pony embroidered on it.

Rachel looks around for a place to throw it away at. On the bench two benches behind them in the corner three middle-schoolers are making out. Rachel says she feels like a chaperon. Gina says she got her first hickey at a skating rink. Gina and Rachel are the oldest ones there easy. They get up and Rachel goes whoa. Gina grabs her wrist in almost the last second. They make their way to the rink. A crystal ball rotating and casting multicolored shafts of sparkling light is hung up in the middle. A boy and a girl go by them. The boy is skating backwards in front of the girl. He has his hands on her hips. She has her hands on his shoulders. Gina asks if Rachel is ready. Rachel says she is. It turns out Rachel is pretty good, just not that good. Her shin muscles or whatever start to hurt pretty soon. Gina looks like a fish in water. Rachel watches her from the side. Gina pumps her fist as she goes by. Gina can go backwards as good as forwards and still do this maneuver she calls criss-cross applesauce. Gina used to be able to do this one move where you crouch down, skate on one foot and stick the other foot out in front of you. Gina is having a wonderful time. She feels glorious. She races some of the kids. She feels like a kid herself. They play I Love Rock 'N' Roll by Joan Jett and the Blackhearts. Everybody stomps their skates to the beat and to the song so so does Gina. The wind or air is not flowing through Gina's hair because she does not have long, flowing hair. Gina's hair is more short and thick and wavy sort of. She comes up from behind and puts her hands on Rachel's shoulders, who is out skating again. She pushes Rachel around the rink once. Then they go to the concession stand. Gina gets an orange drink. Rachel gets a diet. They split a popcorn with extra butter flavoring. They sit down, but not on the same bench as before. You can sit on any bench you want. Gina and Rachel are wore out, especially Gina. She takes off her sweatshirt. She has a t-shirt on underneath with a picture of Droopy on it. She says she is hot. Their bag of popcorn is almost already empty. It went down fast. They talk about stuff and work and what a dick Jon their boss from work is or at least can be. Then they decide to not roller-skate anymore and to go once they finish their drinks. Gina says she already did. She says she had not had orange drink in years. Gina loves orange drink.

    They go home back to Gina's. Gina is about to get out of the car. Rachel says she will see her on Monday morning bright and early. They start at 7 a.m. Gina says to come in for a sec. They go inside. Droopy scrambles up to his feet. He was sleeping right there in the middle of the kitchen floor. Gina laughs and pets Droopy and lets him go out in the back yard to do his business. Rachel wants to know what is up and if it is about the dating service. Gina says it is not about that. She says that it is actually about her boob and that she wants her to feel this spot on her boob. Rachel is surprised. She was not expecting it to be about Gina's boob. Gina reaches up back under her shirt and undoes her bra and works it off and pulls up her t-shirt so her boobs flop out. Nobody can see in through the window from where they are standing. Gina says it is right here on her left boob. She says right here. She takes Rachel's hand and leads it to the spot. Gina asks if she feels that. Rachel says she actually does. That bums Gina. Gina was hoping it had gone away. Rachel says it is probably just a fatty deposit or something. She says she has heard a lot about these fatty deposit things. Gina says that is what the doctor said it could be, too. Rachel asks if Gina already went to the doctor. Gina says yes. Gina pulls her shirt back down. Rachel asks Gina if she told her daughter about it. Gina says she has not. Rachel says she should since she is a nurse. She says that that would be like a second opinion. Gina says she knows but that she does not want to worry her daughter. Gina says she is having a biopsy done this week. Rachel's eyes get kind of big. Rachel hugs Gina. She says everything is going to be okay and that it is most likely nothing or just that fatty deposit. Rachel leaves. Gina goes to the window. She sees Droopy out there. He is squatting down trying to poop. Droopy has problems pooping because he does not drink enough. Then Gina finally sees something coming out. She is relieved. Droopy will get his treat. Then Gina starts to cry.

***

His name is Brooks. He is almost 6 foot. He is looking to settle down with the right woman. If she cooks for him, he will clean his plate every time. He is a hands-on man. He has a special story to tell if she wants to hear it. Gina does and yawns. She cannot believe it. She is still in her pajamas. Gina has not even had breakfast yet. She likes warm cereal best. She heats it up in the one microwave discussed earlier. But on Sundays Gina always fries eggs and bacon. She goes whole hog. She does not even buy the lean bacon or the free-range pork. Sometimes you just have to go whole hog. If you never go whole hog, life will pass you by. Then it will be too late. Then you will wish you had gone whole hog while you still had the chance. It is a Sunday tradition she keeps with herself. Traditions by yourself are not as special as traditions you share with others, but they are still okay. Droopy gets into it. He loves the smell of bacon. He even wags his heavy tail. Gina's pajamas are really just gray sweatpants and her old softball t-shirt from back before she threw her shoulder out. Gina played third. She fired bullets to first whenever a grounder was hit to her. Gina wonders what the special story could be. You know that is why he put it in there to make you wonder. That is kind of smart. She wonders if he is handicapped or almost drowned once. Gina hopes he did not just catch a giant bass and got his picture in the paper. Gina does not know why guys like fishing so much in the first place. Gina wonders why he wrote her at like two in the morning because it tells when the people write you. She wonders if he maybe lives in an earlier time zone because he did not put where he lives. She wonders what he looks like because there is no picture of him and wonders if that has to do with the special story. Gina thinks he could have acne scarring. They can remove those things with lasers nowadays. If he wanted the procedure done, she could accompany him down to the university clinic which is like an hour away and wait for him. They could go eat somewhere. He seems very nice and hungry. He could maybe fix her front door.

You can tell Gina is pretty psyched even if she was all I do not care to Rachel. It makes Gina feel unworthy, but she hopes Brooks is not in a wheelchair. She does not want to push him around all the time. They would have to put in ramps and everything, and maybe those rails in the shower. But then Gina wonders why would he say he is six foot if he was in a wheelchair. That is what pretty much settles it for Gina, how that Brooks cannot be in a wheelchair. Her armpits start to sweat like they always do when she gets excited. She clicks on Reply. She could type like over 60 words a minute if she knew what all to say. She would call Rachel but does not want to tick Chase. She wishes Rachel had a different boyfriend or else that Chase was different. She needs to wake up Droopy. Her heart races like mad. She types thanks and that it is nice to meet him and provides more personal information about herself. Then that is all she types and replies. Then she logs off and goes and wakes up Droopy. He is sleeping in front of the TV. It is not on or anything. He gets right up on his four short legs and is happy to see Gina. Gina tells him the big news. Droopy seems happy and uncomprehending about the news and runs to the back kitchen door. Breakfast is ready by the time Droopy comes back in. He about goes wild when he smells the bacon. Gina gives him a long piece of crispy bacon and tells him he has to eat his other food, too. Gina takes a shower and remembers her dumb boob again. Otherwise Gina is in a kick-butt mood. She puts on her best jeans and the one shirt with the snaps.

She drives to church. You can see it from off the interstate if you know where to look. It used to be the Log Kitchen Barbecue Pit that people liked to stop at and go to. There is always a yellow school bus out in front that does not run that they used to use for outings. Cody is preaching today. He is preaching about money myths. She says hi to everyone, and everyone says hi to her. It is a friendly group. She is about to sit down in the circle. They all say for her to grab a donut. Gina asks if there are donuts. They say they are right over there behind her on the card table. Gina turns around and says mmm and also says thanks. They say she must be controlled by evil forces for her to overlook the donuts. Everyone knows Gina and donuts. Gina says she guesses she is a little out of it this morning. But there is no way she is going to tell them why, though. Gina goes to grab the one with icing and grains on top and filling in the middle, but first asks if anyone wants it, and since nobody does and that she should go for it, that is the one she takes, plus a napkin. Gina sits down on a folding chair in the circle. They talk about the weather and if anyone heard about the accident those kids were in the night before. The kids were from the next town over but had the accident in their town. Liquor was involved. They had been racing around like bats out of heck. Steve says it happened in the middle of the night. Steve knows because he listens to the police scanner. He says they say one kid might not make it. He says they were flown out in the middle of the night. Dana says she thought she heard some noise in the middle of the night. Eddie is Dana's husband. He says Dana is always up in the middle of the night using the restroom and waking him up in the middle of the night. Cody says how what they are talking about fits in well with his theme of the day.

The theme of the day is money matters and is more pertinent than ever in these times of downward spirals, financial trouble, and job turmoil. First he has them all do a general prayer where Cody prays that the Lord will help him speak His Word. Then Cody gets right into the meat of the matter of the subject. It is an intensely practical subject, and everyone listens intensely. Cody hands out a printout with some verses from the Bible dealing with money. Cody says there are 1600 verses in the Bible that concern themselves with money and finances. Dick in the circle says whoah and how that ain't too shabby. Dick likes to use the word ain't, even though he knows it is improper speech. Dick has the insurance business in town. Cody says not to worry and that he is not going to talk about tithing. He addresses Timothy chapter 6 where it says that the love of money is the root of all evil, which is verse 10. He says they have it right there on their printout and so they do not have to flip through their Bibles. Cody says that verse 18 says to be rich in good deeds instead and to be generous and willing to share. This is when Cody takes the opportunity to thank Linda again for footing the donuts, and everyone else thanks her too again. Linda is like, no biggie because her sister works there and gives everyone a thumbs-up.

Cody nods his head and delves right back into his theme. He debunks three prevalent myths about money. A myth is a traditional or legendary story that usually explains some practice, rite or phenomenon or other. Gina listens real close to the first myth and tries not to get any of the cream filling on her lap. Cody talks in a secular, economics way about the myth of the self-made man. Cody says many people do work hard and do make wise decisions and do deserve what they have. Cody says he is the first person to acknowledge that. But then Cody goes on to say that many people do the very same, yet still do not have very much or anything at all. That is the typical Cody curve-ball and is why most everybody likes Brother Cody, except for some people who are never satisfied with anything and are not here today. Cody mentions how they were just mentioning accidents just a moment ago. He says there are many accidents in the life of a human being that leads one person to have more or less than another person does. Gina fits the rest of her donut in her mouth and wipes her mouth. Cody says he is talking about the accidents of your race, your family, your country, and something else Gina does not catch. Gina thinks it might be health, but it might not be. Everybody in the circle knows how Cody did some missionary work in Africa before taking roost with their church. That is why everybody believes Cody when he says that some of the most industrious working people he ever met and who were prudent in their handling of money were people who live on $2 a day and how that they had no chance to get more or amass prosperity solely because of where they were born, the scarce natural resources around them, and the misguided policies of their governments. That is how Cody debunks the first myth, that of the self-made man.

Gina finds it highly enlightening and drifts off mentally as Cody debunks the other two myths. Gina's eye keeps wandering off towards the donuts. She would like to get up and get another donut, but nobody else is. If somebody else does, she will, too. The problem is nobody else is. Finally, Cody's good and soothing talking is over, and everybody gets up and shakes hands and goes over to the donuts. Gina is in heaven. Church goes on all day today. Gina says she will be unable to stay today. Everybody asks why. Everybody likes Gina. Everybody knows how much she likes lunch. Today they are having tater tot casserole. Gina says it is because of Droopy. She says Droopy is not feeling good. She says he needs some TLC and maybe a vet. Everybody understands. Everybody knows how much she likes Droopy and how important Droopy is in her life.

She gets in her car and starts it and drives to a discount department store. It is a huge big box. There is so much stuff there. They have everything. Gina pushes a cart around and looks around. She takes things off the rack and holds them up to her in front of a mirror. Some things look real good at first but then do not look so good once she holds them up to her. Gina goes for a ¾-sleeve knit top with like these stalks or reeds on them. It has a ruched V-neckline, whatever ruched means. It is washable polyester and spandex and imported. Gina cannot resist the side-elastic stretch pants that resist stains and wrinkles. They go good with the top. Gina gets a neckwrap. That is a first for Gina. Gina is more the flannel shirt type. She buys shoes. She wishes she did not walk by the pharmacy. It makes her think of her stupid boob again. Her stupid boob is starting to ruin everything.

After you check out, there is a food court where you can eat. Gina does. She is hungry. It is convenient. Gina does not feel like cooking today. She looks in her bags. She also got a 6-piece snack-pack of assorted natural rawhide for Droopy. That will keep Droopy happy and awake. Gina eats a bowl of chili and a side of apple sauce. She refills her orange drink and takes it with her and drives home. On her way home she stops for gas. She makes some turns, then turns right on Fleet. Fleet is her street. She has lived there her whole life. She passes the one rusted-out truck on blocks that has been that way forever and that some people have been trying to get hauled away or at least covered up with a tarp, but the people keep refusing because it is their driveway. What is wrong with some people? Then she sees her house on the left and a man standing in the carport. He has his back turned to her. He looks like he is examining that one loose piece of siding. Gina pulls in to her driveway. The man turns around. He is tall. He is Brooks.

***

The lunch bell buzzer or horn thing goes off that has to be so loud so that everybody in the factory can hear it. Rachel goes that Gina has to tell her everything about what happened. She can hardly wait. Gina can hardly wait, too. They unpack their lunches. They eat right at their desks. That is where they always eat. There is no in-house cafeteria or dining facilities. The office walls are nicely paneled and warped in brown. They always say how it would be nice if there was a window. Gina could hardly wait to tell everything yesterday.

But when Brooks finally left, and Gina called Rachel, Rachel was not home, and their answering machine does not work because Chase busted it and does not want a new one in his house. Rachel wants her to start at the very beginning even though she already heard the very beginning because Gina was able to tell her that much in between working. Rachel has an egg sandwich and a bag of sunflower seeds. She says that is all she needs. Gina does not see how. Gina has like two triple-decker sandwiches and totally starts chowing down.

She chews and says she pulled into her driveway and this man was standing there. She says she somehow knew it might be Brooks. Rachel asks her how in the world she knew. Gina says she just knew. She says it was just a feeling. She says it was just a weird feeling. Rachel agrees that that it is weird. She says it must have effing freaked Gina out. Gina says she was freaked and that she was freaked out. She says she almost pulled back out, but then another car drove by, and then it was too late, and where would she have drove to anyway? She says she thought he was maybe some psycho pervert. Rachel says she would have thought the same thing. She says there are so many gross psycho perverts out there. She has always loved sunflower seeds. Gina says but that right when she was idling in her driveway with her jaw probably down in her lap, that that was when Brooks broke out in this affable smile and gave her this howdy-doody kind of wave and came right out and asked if she was geniepie4724. Gina could hear what he asked because her window was rolled down because by that time it had warmed up real nice. Gina says she was like how in the heck. She says she must have sounded suspicious and that she did not trust him and wanted him gone otherwise she was going to call the police, even though she did not say so in so many words. Rachel says she would of, too. Gina says that that was when Brooks put up his hands in like a do not shoot type of way. She says he apologized and said he was sorry and just took a wild goose chance by searching for Ginas with her last initial that she provided him when she wrote him back in the town she said she was from listed in the phone book on the Internet and that he did not mean to intrude or scare her. Gina says it was just the down-to-earth way he said everything. Gina says he kind of reminded her of how her brother was before he got involved with that militia thing. Gina's brother is also rather tall. Gina has not seen him for a long time. Gina used to love her brother. Now Gina kind of hates him, especially for dissing Mom, and then Mom died, and they never had the chance to reconcile, and now she is gone, and who knows where he is now.

    Rachel wants to know what happened next. She wants to know if Gina took off her seatbelt and got out of the car or what, or if Brooks came up to the driver's window or what. Gina says it was kind of both. She says that she got out of her car and Brooks approached the car pretty much at the same time. She says how Brooks apologized again and said it was just a crazy whim thing he thought he would try, but he would leave and never intrude upon her again if she told him to and if that is what she wanted. Rachel says she still cannot believe it. She is already finished with her sandwich. She wads up her paper bag and hook shots it into the garbage basket. She says two points. Gina says she still cannot believe it, either, and says that that was when Droopy started barking and looking out the front window all excited. Gina says she told Brooks that that was her dog Droopy and that she needed to let him out. She says Brooks turned around and saw Droopy there pawing at the window and said that he loved dogs. Gina tells Rachel that for her that was just like wow. Not all guys like dogs, although most of them do. Gina still has one sandwich to go and then this big brownie. The dough comes in a tube. You unroll it to like a sheet and bake it in the microwave for seven minutes. It is super easy.

    Rachel wants to know what happened next and wants to know if they went inside, or she got Droopy and came back outside or what. Gina says Brooks asked her if she was going to take Droopy out for a walk, and that he even used his name like Droopy was already his best friend. Gina says she sometimes always thought that Droopy could use a man around the house. Rachel wants to know what in the heck Brooks looks like. Gina says she totally forgot to tell her. Rachel says she totally forgot to ask. She says this whole thing is so crazy and out there that it is hard to know what to ask first. Gina totally agrees. She says he really is six foot and thin as a rail and has this leathery kind of skin she noticed right away and now knows how he got it and that she will tell Rachel in a sec. Gina says he had on what looked like a new pair of stiff jeans and a large oval belt buckle, and that he had on a nice pair of work boots. Gina says he is definitely good-looking, and she was sorry all her new clothes were still in the bags in the car. Rachel says it sounds like he is. She asks if they went for a walk, and Gina tells her what they did, and that they did not. Gina says what they did was that she got the bags out of the car and went back to the back door and opened it up, and Droopy jumped out a little bit and made it down the steps, and Gina opened the gate and let Droopy out in the back yard. Gina says Brooks said that Droopy looked like a fine dog. She says she told him that he should of seen him when he was young. Brooks said he bets. Gina says they were standing at the fence watching Droopy standing in the middle of the yard before he sat and then ultimately laid down. She says that was when she remembered she had a treat for him and pulled out the rawhide. Gina says Brooks took one look at the rawhide and said Droopy was going to love that and asked if he could throw it to him. Gina says she said sure. Gina says Rachel should of seen how fast Droopy got back up and ran after that piece of rawhide Brooks threw and told him to go get it and called him boy. Gina says Brooks suddenly looked ten years younger. Rachel asks if she means Droopy. Gina says yeah, that she meant to say Droopy and that Droopy looked ten years younger. Gina says she asked Brooks if he wanted to go sit down out back on the patio. She says she was not about to invite him into the house even though he seemed so nice. Rachel totally agrees. She says she is glad Gina did not let him in the house.

Gina says Brooks said he thought that would be nice and pointed to the one piece of siding he had been inspecting and said that it needed to be replaced. She says they went and sat on the little slab of concrete patio on the folding chairs she has. Rachel knows the ones she is talking about. They are blue and have the cup-holders. Gina says that as they were going into the back yard and she turned around to close the gate that that was when she realized Brooks did not have a car, or at least she did not see it anywhere, and she was like, huh?, and asked him how he got here and where his car was. Rachel thinks that that is pretty weird and wants to know what he said when she asked. She says that he said that the dang thing broke down on his way in to town and that he had it towed to a garage and that it was being fixed at the garage and that the guy drove him over and dropped him off. Gina says she said that that was nice of him and that Brooks agreed that it was. Gina says that by that time they were sitting down facing the back yard and watching Droopy gnawing away on his rawhide. Gina says Brooks said that it looked like he liked it. Gina says she asked him if he had to drive far or where he drove from and where he lived and that she hoped he did not have to drive far on her account. Then Gina asks Rachel if she is ready for this. Rachel asks if she is ready for what. Gina says if she is ready for what Brooks said because she better hold onto her seat. Rachel says she is holding on and to tell her. Gina says Brooks smiled and said Africa. Rachel about flies out of her seat and says Africa. You should see her face. Then Rachel asks Gina if Brooks is black or what.

That is right when the lunch horn buzzes, meaning it is time to get back to work. Their boss comes walking through the office right on the buzz. He is the one they think is a dick or at least can be. He is wearing a hardhat, meaning that he was inspecting something down on the shop floor. Rachel always says Jon always acts so tough when he gets to wear a hardhat. He says it is time to get back to work and taps his pencil or pen on Gina's desk. He walks through the front office and goes into the back office, which is his office.

Rachel is dying to know the answer to her question. She cannot imagine or picture Gina with a black man. Rachel whispers over to Gina to tell her if he is black or what. Rachel and Gina are the only two in the office because Carol is on vacation this week. She went to the Grand Canyon with her husband. Her dream has always been to go to the Grand Canyon. Rachel told her not to fall off before she left. Jon comes back out of his office. He says he will be gone the rest of the afternoon or maybe just part of it. He says they need to get to work. Then he leaves. Rachel gives him the finger behind his back. Jon totally does not even notice.

Gina says he is not African or black or whatever and says where he said he drove in from yesterday, which is not Africa, but is still pretty far. Rachel wants to know why she said he said Africa for then. Gina holds up her finger to indicate she wants to finish chewing the rest of her brownie. Gina swallows and explains the whole thing. It is an amazing and uplifting story. She talks for like twenty minutes nonstop. Gina says that that was the special story he was referring to when he wrote back to her profile. Rachel is really stunned and amazed. She says wow or whoah or jeez or shit like ten times during Gina's story of Brooks's story, especially at the part where he gets malaria and had to be rescued by flying doctors. Rachel asks how long he was there. Gina says he was there almost ten years, counting the work he did in Malawi. She tells Rachel to look what he gave her. She reaches down under her desk to get her purse and whacks her head on her desk on her way back up. Rachel asks if she is okay, and Gina rubs her head and says she is. She pulls out a colorful bracelet made out of beads and shows it to Rachel. Rachel is amazed and calls it beautiful. Gina says it is a Masai bracelet. She says Brooks got it from when he built a well in a Masai village and a school. She rubs her head again. Rachel asks again if she is okay. Gina says she is okay again.

      Rachel says to put it on, and Gina puts it on. Rachel says it looks beautiful on her and that she should wear it. Gina does not want to wear it because she does not want to break it. She is afraid of breaking it. Rachel says it will not break. Gina says she is probably right, but that she still does not want to wear it yet and puts it away, but admires it once more before she puts it away. Rachel pops the big question and wants to know how long he stayed at her house for, or if he even maybe stayed overnight. Rachel gets this grin on her face when she says overnight and makes the word sound wavy and sexy. Gina says no. She says he did not. She says he stayed until almost eight p.m. and then left. Rachel asks if Gina drove him to pick up his car. Gina says she wanted to and offered like about ten times, but that Brooks refused. She says he said he would rather walk and stretch his legs. She says he said that he was so used to walking after living in Africa for so long. Gina says he said that he does not like driving that much anymore and still has to re-adjust to living in a first-world country. She says that for him things like heating and air-conditioning, refrigerators and malls and everything is really weird. Rachel says that that must be weird for that to be weird. Gina agrees. She says that Brooks has not even been back a month and that everything is still so new and weird, even the food. Gina says Brooks is accustomed to eating goat. Rachel did not know that you can even eat goat, but she guesses you can. Rachel wants to know if Gina ever served any food or beverages. Gina says yes. She says that after that whole story about Africa, she decided to invite him in for lunch and that Droopy came in, too. She says she just put out some lunch meat and buns and some dips and some chips and stuff. She says Brooks petted Droopy while she got everything out. Gina says Brooks said he was still surprised to be back since he thought he would never come back. Rachel asks why he came back then. Gina says because the organization he was working for ran into funding problems.

Every now and then a phone rings, but it is never anything really important. The only important time is when the nurse says Gina can come in tomorrow for the biopsy after all. Gina says that all she knows is that he is back and wants to make roots here and maybe start a helping project here. Rachel asks what Gina means by make roots and if Brooks does not have any roots or something or what. Gina tells Rachel that Brooks does not really have any family and that his parents both passed away before he went to Africa. That was part of the reason why he went to Africa. Rachel thinks that must be terrible when she thinks about her own roots and how important roots are. Gina agrees and says that she likes roots, too, except for her stupid brother. Rachel thinks that must be the reason why he wants to settle down. Gina says yeah. Rachel asks Gina where Brooks is staying at, or if he drove all the way back to from where she said he drove from. Gina says Brooks said he is staying at friends of friends of people he worked with in Africa. Rachel asks Gina if and when they are planning to see each other again, or if she wants to or not. Gina says yes. She says after work.

***

Gina looks at her watch. She is sitting on a green park bench. Lots of people carved their names in it or to fuck off. A lady comes over and puts a flower down at the memorial angel. The memorial angel is in memory of children who died or who were stillborn. Gina now thinks it is a bad place to be meeting. It is like a small, little memorial area in the overall park. Gina did not know. She thought it was just a flower garden, but not the memorial flower garden. You can also pay and have a brick laid with your child's name on it or whatever you want to say on it. You cannot say too much since it is only a little brick. The fee goes to help maintain the memorial area itself. Nobody is getting rich on it or anything. It is not a scam. Gina watches another mom come with her little boy. The little boy leaves a stuffed animal on one of the bricks. It is kind of sad. It is a cute looking elephant or hippo. Candles are not permitted on account of them being fire hazards.

Gina wishes she said to meet at the swings or over at the concession stand where they could watch the game and where she could get an orange drink there. Gina has rediscovered her passion for orange drink. She cannot believe she let so much time pass without having any. She thinks you only live once and how fortunate she is to be alive and how the biopsy is going to be negative all the way and how important it is to think positive. Gina tells herself how that she has been given the chance to live and that from now on she is just going to go for it. The statue is called Angel of Hope. She goes up and looks at it closer and reads the plaque because Brooks still is not there and her butt hurts from all that sitting. The plaque gives a kind of history of the whole deal. Gina hears some cheers and turns around and tries and looks over and sees people standing and cheering on the stands. Someone must have scored a run. Then she looks at her watch again and goes back to the bench again and sits down. She sometimes hears some firecrackers that make her jump.

Then some more time goes by, and then there is some movement off down in the trees and sounds of breaking twigs. She hopes it is a deer and prays that some jerk does not step up out of nowhere and shoot the dang thing. But it is not a deer. It is like a patch of moving colors. At first she cannot tell it is Brooks because he is like 500 yards or feet away. But as he gets closer, it definitely is him. Brooks waves. Gina waves back. Brooks is like half African himself, the way he walks all over and knows his way around. Gina almost half expects to see him carrying a gourd full of water on his head. Gina admits that she likes him. He is sorry he is late. He says he had to walk because his car is still not fixed. He says it is the transmission. He explains to Gina what a transmission is and does and how that it basically increases torque and reduces the speed of the output shaft. Gina does not really follow him. She wants to know why you want the output shaft rotating slower than the input shaft. Brooks tries again, talking about the mechanical advantage. At some point Gina makes that one time-out sign quarterbacks always use. She says she just gets gas and that that is about it as far as it goes.

Brooks says before he goes he would like to give her something. Gina asks him if he is going already after he just got here. Brooks says that unfortunately he has to because of his car and because of that those friends of friends of his have to drive him back. Gina looks disappointed. Her shoulders go down. Brooks pulls a copper earring out of his breast pocket. Gina says it is nice and that she is wearing the bracelet he gave her and shows him that she is. Gina is also wearing those new clothes she just bought. Gina tells him he does not have to be giving her stuff all the time. She says she does not have anything for him and that all she ever gave him was that lunch yesterday, which was basically just cold cuts. Brooks says not to worry about it and that the sandwiches were great and asks Gina if she knows what it is. Gina says it looks to her like an earring that might be African, but that for all she knows about Africa it could be something totally else. Brooks says that Gina is right and that it is an earring. But then Brooks says it is not just any old earring. Brooks says it is a special gift presented by the Buduma lake people in western Chad. Gina says that those people do not ring a bell, but that Chad might kind of. Brooks wants to know if Gina wants to know when it is a special gift for. Gina says she would because she would like to learn more about the Bu-whatever people. Brooks says Buduma and that it is presented on the occasion of marriage.

Gina gets instantaneously tingly on the inside and is all what the heck?! Her eyes search Brooks's face for clues of his intentions, clues of something or at least anything. The only thing Gina does notice is a little scar by his one eye she never noticed before. Gina kind of laughs or smiles a nervous kind of laugh or smile. She says it is nice and pretty and copper and says thanks. Brooks says she is quite welcome and asks if Gina wants to marry him. Gina's eyes about pop out of her freaking head. She accidentally swallows her gum she was chewing and gets this coughing fit. Brooks watches her cough and asks if she is okay and that his question probably took her off guard a little bit. Gina is finally able to breathe normal again and clears her throat. She says that she was surely not expecting that. She says that if anything she was hoping they might go out to El Torito's to eat or something like that, but not this. El Torito's has a huge all-you-can-eat buffet. She thinks it costs either $5.99 or $6.99. That includes a soft drink.

The copper earring is lying right there on Brooks's leathery palm. Gina does not reach out to pick it up. She thinks that Brooks might think that she means yes. Gina says they just met yesterday. Brooks says he knows they did, but he also says that it just feels right to him. He says that many African peoples get married to people they do not even meet until the day of their wedding. Gina says that that is true, even though she never heard about that custom before. Brooks says for her to listen real quick because he has to go. Gina is like go? She is like now? It is a real unorthodox marriage proposal. Brooks says because he has been asked to return to Africa. He says it has come as a complete surprise. He says that that is the whole thing. He says he needs to decide this week about it and that otherwise he would not be asking her to get married so fast. She says she sees. Brooks says she is welcome to think about it. He says he has until the end of the week, but that an answer by Thursday would be best. He says for her to take the earring at no obligation. Gina says thanks. She takes it and looks at it and says what she thinks of it and says thanks. Brooks takes out a piece of paper that was also in his breast pocket and gives it to Gina. He says he can give her his number now. Gina says thanks and looks at the number with a different area code.

A car honks its horn three times from somewhere behind the trees. Brooks says that that is his ride and that he has to go. He says if she calls and he is not there to just ask for Jerry and that Jerry will relay the message. Gina just kind of sits there like she does not know what hit her, like it was a ton of bricks. Then Brooks gets up and goes back through the woods the same way he came. He turns back and waves before he enters the woods. Then he vanishes into the woods.

Gina exhales and gets up and goes and gets that orange drink she was thinking about and hopes the concession stand has. It does. She gets it and goes and sits up on the bleachers. She asks a lady what the score is, and she gives her the whole low-down, that it is tied and in extra innings. The lights flicker on and the diamond lights up. Gina sits there swatting mosquitoes and watching one of the longest games in town history that does not end until the 17th inning. Haystack Pizza ends up beating Noe's Bar by two runs.

***

Her house looks so much different. It is amazing what a hands-on man can do. Tonight is tuna casserole. Gina is pushing it around on her plate with her fork. She is making figure eights with it or the infinity sign. Gina is hungry, but yet she is not. Brooks sure was. He was very or extremely hungry. He asked for more. He hardly came up for air. He wolfed everything. He had no time for figure eights or infinity. It is made of noodles, can tuna fish, cream of mushroom soup, and other choice ingredients. It is a cinch to make. You just throw everything together and pop it in the micro if you have one. It works real good with left over Thanksgiving turkey, but that is not for another two months. Gina checks her wig Image behind her ear to check and make sure it is still on and not slipping off the side of her head somewhere. It features all-over barely curled layers.

Brooks finished painting the house today. It looks wonderful, gorgeous, and light mauve, a color sometimes referred to as pale lavender. The last room was the hallway and bathroom. He worked until like two in the morning last night because Gina knows because she heard the roller going back and forth across the walls all night. At like midnight she peeked her head out her bedroom door and asked him how much longer he had. At like one she asked him to just finish tomorrow, which was in fact today. The phone keeps ringing again.

Gina just sits there letting it ring because she knows who it is. She knows her daughter is letting it ring because she knows her mom is home and just not picking up. After like more than 100 rings, because she counts, Gina almost screams and throws her fork at the phone that leaves a speck of casserole on the freshly painted wall. Gina rarely if ever throws things in anger. Something is clearly wrong with Gina.

Gina picks up the phone but does not say anything. Gina's daughter does not say anything either. They each just sit there breathing and fuming into the phone. Then she asks her if she told him yet, but then says she knows she did not before she even has a chance to answer the question. Then she just goes apeshit on her like every time. She asks what the eff is up with her and especially that Brooks dude she has not even effing met yet and who married her mom after like one day, and generally the whole effing marriage shit. Gina's daughter is very upset. Otherwise she would not use that kind of language because she knows her mom does not appreciate that kind of language. Gina says she is not going to talk to her if she continues to use that kind of language. Gina's daughter says she knows and apologizes for the language. Then they go back to sitting there fuming in silence. Then Gina asks her daughter what it is she really wants to know because she no longer even knows what it is she knows and does not know. That gets the whole apeshit going again. Gina hangs up and picks up the fork laying down on the floor at her feet. She goes over to the sink and grabs some Lime-A-Way so she can try and remove the small casserole stain. From the window over the sink is where Gina saw Droopy dead like just three weeks ago. Droopy was just lying there in the grass in an uncommon position for him. Gina immediately sensed the worst. She squirts some Lime-A-Way on the stain and rubs it gently with a paper towel. Gina also has Brillo pads which would work but which would tear the drywall to shreds.

Michelle calls right back. Gina is pretty much the only one who still calls her Shelly. Like her nametag at work reads Michelle. This time Michelle does not wait and sit there in silence and fume. She says right off the bat that she just wants to talk this thing through to where it needs to be so that they can just be adults and get to the bottom of this thing. Gina says she likes the sound of that better because otherwise she is going to disconnect the phone, which Michelle knows she never would. The Lime-A-Way works even though it is intended for use on lime, calcium, and rust stains. Michelle says in a caring tone that comes out of nowhere that it is just that she is worried about her, and that that is all. That opens up the flood gates. Gina starts to cry. The conversation is all over the page, first the screaming and yelling, now the tears. It is hard to understand her because she is crying and trying to talk at the same time. It makes for odd, sometimes scary sounds. But it sounds like Gina says that she does not know what to do anymore and that she does not want to die.

Michelle reacts by acting like a nurse. She says that first of all she is not even going to come close to dying. She repeats the not even close part. She says because she knows because she contacted her oncologist. Gina wipes her nose on the paper towel she still has in her hand. She is careful not to wipe it on the part where the Lime-A-Way is. It could sting or burn. Gina asks if she really did. Michelle says she really did. Michelle says that the hair loss is common but will grow back in time. She says it only makes it look like you are dying but you are really not. Gina does not have a cordless phone, but her cord is just long enough if she kind of stretches for her to reach the trashcan and throw the paper towel away. They talk about the wig for a while. Gina is starting to sound like her old self again, the one without cancer and the one without a new inscrutable husband. Like they hardly do anything together. One time they went out to the ice-cream place and had shakes. Gina got fudge, and Brooks got a marvel, even though that is not technically a shake. Gina tells Shelly that she hangs it up on her bedpost before going to sleep. She says it looks like a mop up there. That gets them both laughing.

That gets Michelle back on track. She tells her mom she has finally got to tell Brooks about her illness no matter what. Gina says he just left. He left through the front door, which is another thing he fixed and that works now. Michelle says it totally blows her effing mind, and then she corrects herself and says it totally blows her mind big-time that Brooks does not know her mom has breast cancer and that her mom never told him yet. Gina says she knows. She says she knows she should of. She says it is tearing at her with guilt. What Michelle wants to know is how he could possibly not know. Gina says she knows what she means. Michelle says she knows that her boob must be all marked up with lines for the radiation therapy. What Michelle basically means and is getting at is if he has ever seen her naked or been intimate with her yet or not, and if so, then how come no one said anything about the lines on her boob, and if not, then how come. Gina knows exactly what she is getting at and thinking, but does not say anything. Gina just says that everything happened so fast and that Brooks is always so dang busy working on the house all the time, which is great on the one hand and helpful, but on the other hand, and that otherwise Brooks is not much of a conversationalist, is how Gina puts it. Michelle keeps at it. She is in relentless mode. This whole thing has been nagging at her since it the day it started, or at least the day it started for her when her mom called and told her and Michelle was like what the eff. Michelle asks her if Brooks finally ever got his car back from the shop or what ever happened to the mystery car, or if he still walks everywhere or what, and how he gets all the supplies home to work on the house without a truck, and if he even has a job. Gina just says no. That is literally all she says. Michelle repeats what Gina just said. Gina says she does not know. She says she is at work all day and that when she comes home the front room suddenly has like new carpet, for example. Then after no one says anything, Michelle says she can finally have off next week and is coming no matter what, and Gina does not say anything. That means she really wants her to come this time and hopes she does and will worry later about where she will sleep since Brooks usually sleeps on the waterbed, which Gina first thought was strange and still does, or else goes out for all-night walks.

Gina picks absently at where the little spot was on the wall and still cannot believe what she did. She does not mean throwing the fork. Gina sometimes thinks if she would just get really sick and almost die, but not die, and have to be in the hospital for like a month, that that would be a lot better than how things were now because then everything would be out in the open and he would at least know and maybe not get mad at her for not saying anything since she is the one who almost would of died, and then they could just laugh the whole thing off as a royally bad idea and get divorced, and she would gladly reimburse him for all the work he did on the house and for taking care of Droopy's remains for her. These are just Gina's private thoughts, though, because they already hung up about five or ten minutes ago. She could never share thoughts like these with her daughter and can hardly admit them to herself. Some of the repairs Brooks did besides repainting the interior and fixing the front door are: fixing that one piece of vinyl siding by the carport, replacing the mailbox with one with a flag that does not always fall down, getting rid of the musty basement smell by first mopping the floors with bleach, then sealing all cracks in the walls and floor with hydraulic cement, and then installing a dehumidifier, putting down new carpet in the front room, and fixing nearly all the floor squeaks. There was other stuff, too, like relining the kitchen drawers with colorful lining paper, redoing the front lawn, and she thinks Brooks might be the one who finally got that guy up the street to remove that eyesore truck.

***

The next week cannot go or come fast enough. Gina really wants it and her daughter to finally just be here. It is like she just cannot stand it anymore, just cannot breathe. Brooks is real anxious about meeting her. He comes home one day with a haircut. His mustache is gone. He keeps asking Gina what exact day she is coming and what time. Gina can tell him the day just fine, but not the time. It depends on what time her daughter leaves as to what time she gets there.

Gina asks Jon for half a day on that Thursday so she can get a few things ready for when Shelly gets there. Thursday is the big day. Jon is like sure, no prob, go ahead, be my guest. That is the thing with Jon. Sometimes he can be so understanding and accommodating, and other times he is just your typical asshole. It is like he is a psycho or something, which is Rachel's take on him. Rachel is working away. The end of the month is always a busy time for a bookkeeper. Carol is back in the office. That means Rachel and Gina do not get to gossip as much as they do when she is on vacation or home with one of her seizures. It makes them feel bad and all and everything, but the office climate is just way better without her. Meanwhile, Gina performs menial tasks, like manning the phone. Sometimes when either she is so busy and caught up in her menial tasks and loses track of time or else is so dazed from the radiation, she will say good morning on the phone when it is already afternoon, but usually she gets it right. It is not all that hard.

Gina waits for Carol to leave for lunch break. Carol always goes out to eat because she thinks she is better than them is what they think. Carol leaves, and Gina reaches under her desk to get her bag. This time she does not bump her head like she did that last time. Rachel asks if she is all excited and has lots to do. Gina says she is. She says she is just going to buy some cold cuts and buns and that that way everybody can just do their own thing. She already has pretty much every condiment you could ever want at home so all she needs is the cold cuts and the buns. She says she is also getting a cake. Rachel wants to know what kind. Gina tells her the size and says it is going to say Shelly on it in icing because they are having some special that if you put your or someone special's name on it, it is like 15% off. Gina tells Rachel that she asked them that if she had two names put on it if it would be like 30% off, but just as a joke. Rachel says that that would have been cool because after like seven or eight names you could get a free cake. Then she goes after even less than seven, so like six.

Gina goes to the store she always goes to and gets what she needs to get. She is able to stick to what is on her grocery list and not stray from it and get a bunch of stuff and food she does not need and like and only spoils and turns green or fuzzy. Gina feels special today as she pushes her cart up and down the aisles. It is a good, weird feeling. She does not even feel like Gina. She opens the trunk the old-fashion way and puts the bags in her trunk. One of these days she is going to have to get in there and really see what all is in there and clean it up. Gina stares up for a moment at the big, blue, cloudless sky and takes a big, deep breath. Way over there there are a couple clouds she does not regard. It is sort of like a family reunion, only that there are basically only three people in the whole family. So they cannot even get a good friendly game of bags or washers going. But you play the cards you are dealt with. You deal with it. You push up your sleeves like Gina always does with her sleeves and get on with things. Gina closes her trunk twice because it never latches the first time and returns her cart to where you are supposed to bring them when you are done.

Gina has to take a small detour on her way home because of roadwork. It is no big deal. Then at the stop sign she turns onto Fleet. That is when everything starts to take a turn for the worst. The first block is no big deal. The one rusted-out truck is gone. So that is actually good, but not news. Then Gina's driveway comes into view. It is on the left. She is like whose car or truck is that in her driveway? Is that finally Brooks's mystery car or truck? Or did Shelly get a new one or truck she never told her about and wanted to surprise her with? That could be. But who is that family standing around? Gina is driving pretty slow to have all these questions. She has to park on the street in front of the mailbox. If the mail carrier comes and she is still blocking the mailbox, she will just have to run out and get it herself.

Gina gets out of her car and hitches up the back of her jeans by a belt loop. Everybody is like all hi and hey and howzit goin. The mom in the family nudges her two children who look like they are in grade school to be polite and say hi. Gina asks if she can help them. That is so Gina. She always wants to help. The two kids are hanging tight to their mom. She tells them not to step on the nice new grass and that the back yard is for playing. The two children run off and are told to close the gate behind them. Gina sort of instinctively raises her hand, but not really like she is raising an objection or anything. It is more like an instinctive response when you see people you have never seen before suddenly running all over your property without permission. But the dude is like nope as to the help question, saying that he just thought they would drive on by with the kids after school and surprise them. The response does not seem logical or even sane to Gina. Then he goes if she is looking for someone. That totally throws Gina, who is otherwise not thrown very easy. Because are you ever looking for someone when you pull up and park at your own curb? Then it hits her and she gets it and is like they must be the people Brooks has been staying with and telling her about. But the dude goes that he does not know any Brooks. He adjusts his hat and asks his wife if she does, and Shae says she does not, and he jokes that she damn better not. You can just tell the dude is in a real good mood, as is Shae. He kind of pulls her over to him and puts his arm around her. She slips a hand into his back pocket. She is wearing a t-shirt that you can see where her little boobies are. Ever since the thing with her own boob Gina has been paying more attention to other people's boobs. She only has three more treatments to go.

Shae goes that it is a very nice neighborhood. She says the kids are thrilled to have a yard finally. Gina says it is. She says she has been living there her whole life. The dude asks whereabouts, and Gina goes right here. She kind of kicks the driveway with the toe of her shoe while pointing with an open hand towards the house. It almost looks like she is playing that game charades. She says that this right here is her house. The dude is like what is that supposed to mean and that they just bought this house this morning. His arm falls from his wife's waist. Gina gets a silly grin, and she says something you always hear when mix-ups like this occurs. She goes there must be some mistake. She says that this here is her house and that here is her key right here. She has been holding her keys the whole time since getting out of the car so it is real easy to show them her key. The dude then says sorry. He calls her lady because he does not know her name. He says that they just bought this house this morning and that he has the deed to prove it. You could not really say there is animosity in his voice. He is simply laying claims to his rightful property. It is a big day for him, too, to finally own a house and to give his kids a better life than he had. Gina goes that there must be some mistake again. Gina is in such a state of utter perplexity and starts walking farther up the driveway. The dude asks her where she thinks she is going. Shae tells Ritchie to keep cool, Ritchie being his name. My goddamn house is how he puts it to her and adjusts his cap again.

Gina asks if they are sure they have the right address and states the address, including city and zip because maybe they are in the whole wrong city. But Ritchie is able to tell her how many square feet the lot has, what direction it faces, and where the water meter can be found. He knows his stuff. He reaches in to his truck and produces the deed. He says right here. Gina goes like what is that. Ritchie tells her. He is bringing it on. Shae says Ritchie. Gina takes a closer look at the document and nearly falters. Shae reaches out and briefly grabs her elbow. Shae's sinewy arms are covered with freckles. Shae can perceive imminent danger. That comes from her job. Gina does not bother with all the law gibberish. She just focuses in on the address typed in bold across the top. She just sees the names of the two parties. She asks Ritchie if he is the Richard. He says since the day he was born. Shae gives him that look, and he goes what? Gina wants to know who Perry Harris is. Shae says that that is the gentleman who they bought the house from. Gina repeats her same old line again, the one about how there must be some kind of mistake. Ritchie goes tall dude and indicates about how tall. Gina says but. That is all she is able to say. The children call out to their mom to come see this cool thing they found. Gina starts digging in her pocket for her phone.

Brooks does not answer. Gina calls Rachel and tells her to come over right now. Rachel wants to know what is wrong because she can tell something is way wrong. Gina says just to come. Rachel

The Dark Continent

says she is out with Chase and to hold on. It sounds like she covers her phone and has this conversation with Chase. Knowing Chase, he probably does not want to go. Shae puts her hands in her back pockets and walks up to the backyard fence to attend to the kids. She works at an animal shelter. Rachel is back on the phone. She wants to know what happened. Gina does not go into detail. She just tells her the bottom line, which takes like four words. Rachel freaks. She tells her not to move and that they are on their way. There is some bullshit noise from Chase in the background.

They get there 30 minutes before Michelle will and a lot louder because of Chase's souped-up car. Rachel finds Gina lying next to her wig down on the new sodding. Rachel screams and asks no one in particular if she is dead. Chase says that she ain't dead. It is true. Gina's hand is pulling or clawing at the grass. Shae had the wherewithal to call an ambulance just in case. Chase says nice truck to Ritchie. Ritchie says 6.8 liter Triton V10 and pops the hood. Their heads disappear underneath it. Rachel kneels down over Gina, repeating her name and asking her to say something. For her part Gina keeps repeating the word fool. Rachel looks up helplessly at Shae who appears saddened at the sight of Gina lying on what is now her front lawn. Rachel asks Shae if they know each other or something, and if it is maybe from aerobics class. They go back and forth about instructors and class times, and it turns out they do. It turns out Rachel is sometimes just getting there when Shae is finishing up. She asks her how she likes the cardio mix.

Nachtmusik

His dad wants to know if he wants to hear a little nachtmusik. It is Cliff's little quip or joke or something funny or humorous to say that Cliff likes to say. Jake says whatever. Cliff fiddles with the stations until he finds a station. Then they listen to that station. Then Cliff asks Jake if Jake likes this song Jump and likes Van Halen or if he ever even heard of Van Halen and the song Jump. Jake is like checking his messages. Cliff tells his son how when he was his age everyone went wild over Jump. He says how everyone went wild over the opening synthesizers and how everybody would jump every time David Lee Roth sang the word, jump. Cliff sometimes still follows Van Halen and where they are touring and who their lead singer is at the moment. Cliff says how it is pretty wild how that Eddie Van Halen has a son named Wolfgang. He says it is pretty wild how Wolfgang plays in Van Halen even though he is still in 12th grade like Jake is. Jake is in 12th grade. Cliff asks Jake if he would like to be on stage with Van Halen right now. Jake says he does not know. He says probably not. Cliff looks surprised and intrigued and baffled. He says no kidding, then makes an unexpected left turn into a convenience store. Jake is like where are they going and how he thought they were going straight home. Jake says he has plans tonight. Cliff says to just hold on and how he wants to pick something up and how he will be right back. Cliff leaves the motor running and runs into the convenience store. Convenience store doors always open both ways.

That is part of what makes them so convenient and also easy to rob. Cliff charges through the doors and looks for what he is looking for and finds it. Then he comes back out with what he was looking for and found and puts the bags back in the backseat. Cliff gets all situated behind the wheel and fastens his seatbelt before his car tells him to, which is technically his wife's car. Cliff hates it when his wife's car is always telling him what to do. Cliff says hey and if Jake changed the station or something. Jake says yeah, and Cliff says he loves NPR. Jake says they have to listen to it two hours a week for class. Cliff wants to know what class, and Jake says honors. Cliff says that sounds like a good class. He says it sounds way better than psych or something. Then Cliff backs out. Cliff loves Park Assist Rear when he backs out. Park Assist Rear makes it easier for him to reverse. It alerts him with a pulsating tone when he is too close to an object behind his car. Cliff does not hit or run anything over and pulls out into a lane of traffic. Cliff drives, Jake thumbs a message that reads L8, and they both listen to a fascinating report about the three ways that your brain betrays you. Cliff goes huh when he hears that his brain is wired to prevent him from seeing the world as it is. Cliff says wild when they say how he sees patterns where there is only randomness. Cliff asks Jake if he heard that and if he is listening. Jake reads the message he just got that says WRU@ and thumbs ??? and says yeah. Cliff drives by a Kelly Tires and then a Midas dealer like not even 20 seconds later. He says he never saw that there before and asks if Jake ever saw that there before. Then NPR goes on to talk about some German neurologist who coined some term called apophenia. Cliff says how the Germans are notorious for coming up with these long words. Jake gets another message that says WTH and also says WTF???? The German guy says how for example thousands of otherwise healthy, intelligent people believe that the shuffle function on their iPods is broken because they do not think the songs are random enough. Cliff thinks how he has thought the same thing before. He thinks how that makes him otherwise healthy and intelligent. Jake asks him where the hell they are going. Cliff says going? The German guy sums up by talking about pattern detection. He says how that it has been responsible for so much of our species' success, but can just as easily betray us. Cliff says double-edged sword. Then the story is over and a few bars of dissonant jazz come on. Technically, that is when Cliff says going? and then keeps driving down past the donut shop and the Chinese take-out, which are two places to eat located right next to each other, and down the huge hill. Then comes a bunch of windy turns, and then comes the old water treatment plant down by the river bottoms. Jake asks his dad what they are doing. Jake says it is Friday night. He says to come on. Cliff says for him to hold his horses. Cliff says he wants to show and tell him something. Cliff says he thinks this is it. He pulls off onto a gravel road. It quickly ends at a high chain link fence with a No Trespassing sign on it. Jake says it does not look like they should be parking there. Cliff turns off the radio when it starts talking about the national debt. Cliff says how they used to come down there all the time back in high school. The next message Jake gets says NWRU@. Jake responds with IHNI. Jake says Cliff and that he is serious about wanting to get home. Cliff gives him this hang on hand gesture thing. Cliff reaches back to the backseat to get the bags, which is where the bags are. But Cliff cannot reach the bags. Cliff unbuckles his stupid seatbelt that thinks it knows everything and is now able to reach the bags. He yanks the bags up to the front seat. Cliff pulls a six-pack of beer out of the one bag and calls his son champ and asks him if he wants a beer. Jake just won an important race and is now the district champ. Jake set a course record, or CR. Everyone knows Jake will take state, too. Everyone knows he will place in nationals. Jake really is a champ. Cliff is not kidding. Jake is like huh? He is like wh-wh-what? He is like beer? Cliff asks him if he is catching flies because his mouth is open and says that it is only 3.2 and that Mom will never know. Cliff just hands him a beer, and Cliff takes a beer, and then Cliff and Jake sit there and drink beer, father and son. The beer is nice and cold. Cliff turns back on the motor and puts on the heat because it starts to get cold. Then Cliff points with the heel of his bottle and asks Jake if Jake sees those huge tanks over there. Jake is like yeah in a duh kind of way because the huge tanks are right there behind the fence. You would have to be blind not to see the huge tanks. Cliff tells Jake that there are these huge open sludge pools behind the tanks. He says that that is where the city sewage first goes to settle out. Then he takes another big drink. Jake does not say anything. He has never been overly interested in sewage. Jake likes chemistry more. Jake takes another drink, and Cliff takes another drink. Cliff says that back when he was in high school there was a rumor that someone drowned in one of those sludge pools. Jake says it was probably just an urban legend and asks if they can get going now. Cliff asks Jake if he is already done with his beer. Jake says he is. Cliff tells him to just throw it out the door and grab another one. Jake is like if he means litter. Cliff tells him yeah. He says he does not want Mom finding all these bottles lying around and asking questions. Jake lowers the window and tosses out the bottle and raises the window back up, and Cliff hands him another bottle. Cliff takes another bottle. The bottles are twist-off so they do not require a bottle opener. That played a big part in why Cliff bought the specific brand of beer he bought. That and that it is micro-brewed with local ingredients. Then Cliff remembers the Habanero BBQ almonds in the other bag. Cliff loves Habanero BBQ almonds more than any other snack he can think of and takes the can out of the bag and opens the can. He loves how the can makes that zssshhhh sound. Cliff tells Jake to take a handful. He says they are good against the buzz. Jake asks if it would not be better to just go. Cliff asks if he is stupid and says they cannot be driving around with open beer in the car. He turns back down the heat. Then he turns back off the car.

Then he asks Jake if Jake has given any thought to his future. Jake gets a message. This time it is a message accompanied by a picture. The message is HB ;-). The picture is a picture of Samantha with her jeans unbuttoned and wearing a bra. Cliff asks Jake if he has. Jake says to hold on. Cliff wants to know what Jake is doing. Jake thumbs 6Y and MTF?, then asks Cliff what the question was. Cliff tells him to first keep up with the Habanero to make sure he has something in his stomach. Jake takes some more Habanero. Cliff repeats his question. Cliff also wants to know how Jake thinks he will finance college especially if he does not get a running scholarship, which everyone knows he will. Jake stares some more at Samantha. He spaces out on her buttons. Cliff says Earth calling Jake. Jake says huh? Then Jake says oh yeah and how he does not think he wants to run collegiately. Cliff says the fuck?! Cliff tells Jake he just breezed to a CR at districts. Cliff tells Jake that he is a gifted runner, a fast runner, a smart runner. Jake says he knows, but how he does not know. He says he probably just wants to concentrate on chemistry and then go to med school. Cliff does this double-take thing. He is like med school? He is like if he heard right and Jake said med school. Jake says yeah and wants to know what the big deal is about med school. Cliff shakes his head and goes med school and takes a drink. Then after he drinks, he wants to know if Jake wants to go to med school just so he can treat a bunch of head cases like his mom the rest of his life. That really takes Jake by surprise to hear his mom called a head case. Jake like bumbles and fumbles his cell phone around because he is so surprised and drops his cell phone and tries to grab his cell phone before Cliff does. Cliff grabs it first and looks at his cell phone and at Samantha. Jake says to give him back his phone. Cliff asks Jake if that is Mike Jamison's daughter. Jake says that yeah it is. Cliff asks Jake what her name is again. Jake says Samantha. Cliff says oh yeah right and asks Jake if they are going out. Jake shrugs his shoulders because his dad is so old-fashioned about going out and

Nachtmusik

being steady. Cliff says she is pretty hot and that Jake should go for her and gives him back his phone. When Jake gets his phone back, he puts it back in his pocket. Then they drink in silence for a moment and finish their beers. Then Jake ventures and asks his dad what is wrong with Mom. Cliff suppresses some carbonation running up his windpipe or esophagus and says Mom is fine. He says that thing he said about head cases came out wrong. Jake wants to know if it is more than just migraines or something. The phone beeps in his pocket. He is dying to see what Sam looks like this time and hopes she shows him some ass. Cliff tells Jake that it sounds like he got another message. Jake says it does not matter and that it can wait. Cliff says no and that he is not saying that it is more than migraines. Cliff says that if he is saying anything he is saying that it is less than migraines. Jake wants to know what that is supposed to mean less than migraines. Jake has always wanted to know everything. He has always had such a craving to learn. The car windows are fogged up. That is because of the moisture in the car, and since the outside temperature is much lower tonight than the inside temperature of the car, the moisture condenses on the windows. Cliff turns to his left and faces his window and rubs some of the condensation off the window. Then he peers out the window to see what he can see. By now it is dark outside. Cliff is unable to see or discern a thing. But that does not keep Cliff from looking out and peering and searching and avoiding Jake. That gives Jake an opportunity to look at his cell phone. Jake pulls out his cell phone while keeping his eyes on the back of his dad's head. Then Jake moves his own head as little as possible and his hand with the phone as surreptitiously as possible and checks out Samantha. There is this full-length shot of her. Now her jeans are in a puddle at her feet, and she has her index finger on her lips like she is saying oops and how her pants fell down. Jake thumbs T4BU TIC and slips his phone back into his pocket and finishes his beer. Then at some point Cliff feels a hand on his shoulder. He has been making squigglies on the window the whole time. Jake says hey dad and tells him not to cry and that he will get a job soon and that he just needs to keep looking. Cliff says that he is not crying and stops making the squigglies and turns back around to face the darkness and the fog in front of him. They recently changed the clocks, and that is why it is already so dark even though it is not all that late. Cliff says shit and sorry and how he has been hogging the Habaneros the whole time and offers Jake some more Habaneros. Jake tells his dad that he really thinks they should just get going. Cliff asks going where. Jake says home. Cliff says pfff home and how that is a good one. Jake's cell beeps again with an incoming message. Cliff says how that he used to always think that habanero always meant friend whereas it actually just means someone from Havana. Cliff asks Jake if he knew that. Jake says no. Jake is not taking Spanish. Cliff asks Jake if he knows where Havana even is. Jake just says Cliff come on. Cliff says that they might as well finish off the pix-sack first. Cliff actually says pix-sack and not six-pack. Jake wants to know if his dad does not think he has already had enough. Cliff tells Jake not to patronize his father and places a bottle of beer in his hand and tells him he will be right back and gets out of the car to go take a leak. The cool air is refreshing and cool. Jake checks back out his phone. He reads TAFN... FN ;-). Cliff walks to the rear of his wife's vehicle and undoes his pants. It is hard not to think about how Samantha's pants were undone and whizzes on the hubcap. The hubcap makes a tinging or ringing kind of sound and changes tones depending on if you hit it in the middle or towards the rim. It almost sounds like a tune he knows, but that is probably just his brain fooling him again. Jake thumbs KLF :~) AFAIK 2M2H. CUL8R. Cliff gets back in the car and says Jake question. Jake says to hold on because he is still thumbing the message. Cliff kind of leans over to try and see what all the thumbing is about. Jake kind of leans back so his dad does not see. Cliff asks his son if he has another naked girlie on there or something. Jake says she was not naked. Cliff says pretty darn close. He says Jake better hope Mike does not find out about that. Then Cliff waits and then asks Jake if he is done yet. Then Jake says yeah. Cliff says good because he wants to ask him something. Jake asks what. Cliff pauses a moment and then says now he forgot what it was he wanted to ask. That cracks Jake up and spits some beer out of his mouth on account of all the cracking up. It like sprays onto the dash. Cliff tells Jake to stop laughing and not to make a mess in the car because it is Mom's car and then starts cracking up, too. Then they each make each other crack up more. Then Cliff has this idea and takes some of the Habanero nuts and beans Jake. Jake says hey dude then grabs some nuts and pegs his dad back. Soon it is like nuts are flying every which way. It is a Habanero fight and a great time. Cliff and Jake are laughing and saying things like ow and gotcha and nailed your ass. Then before they know it, all the nuts are gone. Cliff leans his head back against the headrest. He is worn out and breathes hard for a second. Then he says how he now has something to do tomorrow vacuum the car tomorrow and punches the horn. Cliff punches the horn a second time and a third time. That gets Jake to finally stop laughing. The horn sounds real loud out there down by the river bottoms, the horn sound traveling through the remaining rustling leaves and out across the black, rippling water. Jake tells his dad he should probably stop doing that. Jake says that they probably do not want to attract attention under the circumstances. Cliff does as he is told and stops. He says he remembers now what he wanted to ask and asks Jake if he knows what a mortgage is. Jake says mortgage, mortgage like he is searching his brain. Cliff says yeah and tells him how it is spelled. Jake says he thinks so maybe. Cliff asks him which one thinks so or maybe. Jake says he thinks so. Cliff says awesome and downs the rest of his beer and tosses it out the door. Cliff tells Jake to down the rest of his beer so they can get the fuck out of there. Jake says he does not think he can down it and asks his dad if he wants it. Cliff says yeah and how it is a shame to waste a good microprocessed beer made with local ingredients. The really weird thing about all this is is that Jake hardly ever sees Cliff drink beer. Cliff hardly ever drinks beer. Cliff drinks the beer and tosses it right out the door since his door is still open and closes the door. Cliff starts the car, and they both fasten their seatbelts. Cliff runs the wipers and flips on the rear window defroster. His wife's car covers all the bases. Cliff turns on the fog and cornering lights set into the front spoiler. He turns on the high-intensity rear fog light to make the vehicle more visible to vehicles behind him. Then Cliff backs out off of the gravel road. The gravel seems to make a lot more noise now than it did before. Cliff asks Jake if he notices that. Jake says bullshit. Cliff and Jake agree not to turn on the radio and to concentrate solely on the road. They agree that that is a good idea. They agree that they can listen to the radio any old time. The car has all these air bags plus an inflatable curtain so Cliff and Jake are pretty safe there. Cliff reaches the blacktop. There is also a whiplash protection system, which is great as well. Now the car drives a lot smoother and quieter. Cliff says he can do this. Jake asks about the radio. Then they both decide again to leave it off. Cliff calls Jake buddy and tells him that he is his co-pilot. Jake says alright and leaves his cell phone in his pocket from now on. Cliff feels comfortable on the swerving road and does not meet any oncoming cars. His hands are firmly set at ten-two. Cliff takes that one big hill no prob. Hills are easy in a car because the car does all the work. The donut shop is closed. Cliff asks his co-pilot if they are doing okay. Jake says all clear. Then they come to the first traffic light and more traffic. The reds and greens and yellows and whites are like moving and shifting and floating disks of kaleidoscopic lights. Cliff is like look at all the lights. Somebody honks behind Cliff, and Cliff begins to drive again. He sets back off at a slow and comfortable pace. Cliff says how there seems to be a lot of traffic for a Friday evening. He says the traffic seems soupier and thicker and warpier than it usually does. Jake is like yeah sure. Jake keeps having to say blinker. The water tower is coming up. It is all lit up and has a blinking red light on top. The more Cliff comes up to the water tower, the more he first sees the big **W** and then the big **Y** emblazoned on the water tower. Then Jake says road, and Cliff quickly repositions himself between the white lines and says good eye. Cliff coasts into the left turning lane. Jake says blinker, and Cliff says on it. Cliff says for some reason he keeps forgetting the blinker. Jake says how it is probably the beer, and Cliff says how it probably is. They idle and wait for the traffic to pass and the light to change. Cliff says god and how in a couple more months it is going to be Christmas again. Jake can already feel Samantha in his arms. She is into biology. Then the light changes. Cliff follows the car in front of him at a safe distance and executes a smooth left turn. Cliff says almost made it now. He says how that should be the last of the left turns. The traffic thins, and some four-way stops follow. Jake says not to forget to drop him off at school so he can pick up his car. His car is at school because he drives to school. Cliff says thanks and how he almost forgot. That makes just one more left turn into the school parking lot. The school parking lot is vast and empty since the football team has an away game and prom is not until next week. Cliff asks which way, and Jake says down to the right. He says to watch the speed bumps. Cliff watches the speed bumps but then goes over a parking lot island. He says shit and what the fuck was that. Jake says it was an island. Cliff says he hates islands and then drives back off the island. Cliff hopes the alignment is not screwed. Jake says how there is his car right up there. Cliff says where, and Jake says right up there, and Cliff says gotcha and keeps driving. With the headlights and the fog lights, Cliff now has a clear and bright side view of Jake's car set against a backdrop of night. Then he keeps driving and approaching, and Jake's car starts to look like two or even three cars the closer and closer he gets to it or them. Cliff is briefly like what is going on and how weird. Jake goes hey and then what the fuck and then stop real loud. Cliff hits Jake's car right around where the gas tank would be if it were on that side. Cliff was lucky he was going slow enough, and none of the air bags open. Jake says you dick you hit my car. Cliff says not to tell Mom. Jake tells Cliff to back up, who does. Jake gets out of the car to go and inspect his car. Cliff stays in the car and leaves the headlights and fog lights on and lets his head fall against the wheel. When Cliff lifts his head back up, he sees Jake is on his phone and hurries up and gets out of his seatbelt and out of the car. Cliff says he better not be calling Mom. Jake covers the other ear he is not talking on and turns the other way. Cliff says not to call the insurance company either. He asks Jake if he is calling the insurance company. Cliff approaches Jake's car. He can see the dent very well because the headlights and fog lights are shining right on it. Cliff runs his hand over the dent. Jake comes back. Cliff asks Jake who he was talking to. Jake says how it is none of his business. Cliff says he hopes it was not Mom. Jake says not to worry about it. Cliff says just a little fender bender. Jake says that he did not hit the fender. Cliff says he knows and says he knows what a fender is. Then they stand around silently in the light of the headlights and fog lights and do not say anything. Cliff digs around in his pockets. Then Jake says fuck man. Then Cliff pulls out a roll of quarters. He says here take this and hands it to Jake. Jake goes to take it and is like what is this because he cannot see what it is. Cliff says money. He says ten dollars. Jake says it is a fucking role of quarters. Cliff says to take Samantha out for pizza on him. Jake says how Cliff sucks and how he is not going to fucking pay in quarters. Jake says he is not a twelve-year-old. Then Jake says how Mom was right and winds back and hurls the quarters into the darkness. A second or two later there is this thud. That means it probably landed on an island. Otherwise it would have landed on the pavement and probably busted open and made all this coin noise.

Jeff Tapia is the author of two plays and short fiction in German and the recipient of an Austrian national writing grant. He grew up in a suburb of St. Louis and works as a translator.